Praise for the Mead Mishaps Series

"One of the freshest voices in fantasy romance! This book has it all: spice, humor, and a world I want to get lost in!"
—Katee Robert, *New York Times* bestselling author

"Sexy, witty, and fun as hell—*That Time I Got Drunk and Saved a Demon* is the instant mood boost we all need."
—Hannah Whitten, *New York Times* bestselling author

"Hilarious, hot, and full of heart, *That Time I Got Drunk and Saved a Demon* is exactly what you need in your life. Right now. Go pick it up because it is the cure to any reading funk and might even clear up acne. I'm serious. It's that good."
—Avery Flynn, *USA Today* and *Wall Street Journal* bestselling author

"A hilarious, down-to-earth romance with magic, adventure, and intrigue. What's not to love?"
—Talia Hibbert, *New York Times* bestselling author

"Perfect entertainment for my stressed-out brain, and I was definitely rooting for those two wacky kids to have their HEA."
—*Smart Bitches, Trashy Books*

T0383023

By Kimberly Lemming

MEAD MISHAPS

That Time I Got Drunk and Saved a Demon

That Time I Got Drunk and Yeeted a Love Potion at a Werewolf

That Time I Got Drunk and Saved a Human

MEAD REALM NOVELLAS

Mistlefoe

A Bump in Boohail

THAT TIME I GOT DRUNK AND YEETED A LOVE POTION AT A WEREWOLF

MEAD MISHAPS: BOOK TWO

KIMBERLY LEMMING

orbit

orbitbooks.net

Copyright © 2022 by Kimberly Lemming
Excerpt from *Half a Soul* copyright © 2020 by Olivia Atwater
Excerpt from *A Feather So Black* copyright © 2024 by Lyra Selene Robinette

Cover design by Alexia E. Pereira
Cover art by Mike Pape
Cover copyright © 2024 by Hachette Book Group, Inc.
Map by @Saumyasvision/Inkarnate
Author photograph by Kimberly Lemming

Orbit
Hachette Book Group
1290 Avenue of the Americas
New York, NY 10104
orbitbooks.net

First Orbit Paperback Edition: February 2024
First Orbit Ebook Edition: May 2023
Previously published in paperback in Great Britain by Jo Fletcher Books, an imprint of Quercus Editions Ltd, in August 2023
Previously published in ebook in Great Britain by Jo Fletcher Books, an imprint of Quercus Editions Ltd, in March 2023
Originally published in paperback and ebook in May 2022

Orbit is an imprint of Hachette Book Group.
The Orbit name and logo are registered trademarks of Little, Brown Book Group Limited.

Library of Congress Control Number: 2023944388

ISBNs: 9780316570312 (trade paperback), 9780316570299 (ebook)

Printed in the United States of America

LSC-C

Printing 5, 2024

THAT TIME I GOT DRUNK AND YEETED A LOVE POTION AT A WEREWOLF

Content Warning

Chapter 1

Brie

Potatoes are by far the most versatile crop. You can fry them up, bake them, or throw them at undesirable men who refuse to leave you alone. At least, that's what I enjoyed doing with them. I snatched another baked potato from my friend Cinnamon, who balked in protest. Before the spice trader could reclaim her favorite treat, I side-stepped out of her reach and prepared to fire another round at my latest annoyance. Jack stumbled back and held his hands up. The splatter of hot cheese and potato on his cheek fell away. In its place was a red mark that swelled with the consequences of him not following my simple instructions. "Leave me alone, Jack. I told you I'm not interested."

The farmer held up his hands, feet widening in a stance as if he was preparing to swat away the offending tuber. "Brie, come on, how much longer are you going to play hard to get?" His crooked mouth turned up into a grin. A forced laugh choked out of his skinny neck before he took a tentative step forward.

Gods, I was so sick of his shit. I looked around, pretending to be confused for a moment. "Jack, have you lost your mind? Did you come here so I could help you find it? I can't think of any other reason me pelting you with tubers would be mistaken for flirting."

Cin stomped her foot. "Not my potato! Throw something else at him!"

My shoulders slumped before I took my gaze off the farmer to reassure my friend and her lewd lust for food. "I'll buy you another one and give you a wheel of cheese. Just let me deal with this asshole."

The annoyance in her features vanished in an instant. Replaced with starry eyes and a wide grin. "Nevermind, it's yours!" she chirped and spun around, set her fists on her hips and glared at the man as if he were a small child in need of a reprimand. "You heard the lady, Jack. She doesn't want you, so get gone." Cinnamon's glare in itself wasn't the most terrifying thing in the world. She herself was rather short. Several inches of her height could be attributed to the proud crown of curls on her head. But what was terrifying was the dragon shifter behind her.

Cin's husband, Fallon, sat on a bar stool, nursing a mug of mead. The obsidian horns decorating his head nearly scraped against one of the many colorful fall banners decorating the stall. He took another sip, before turning to see whatever poor sap angered his wife. Jack's back straightened when the demon locked eyes with him. The farmer's raised hands twitched. He opened his mouth, then thought better of it and swallowed. I couldn't blame him. Fallon was terrifying.

It had only been a short time since Cinnamon and our goddess-chosen hero, Priscilla, returned from their respective journeys. Normally, a returning hero was met with cheer and a village-wide fall celebration to commemorate another successful demon purge. But Cin returning with a merry band of pirate demons (very much NOT purged) and news of our goddess' death put a bit of a damper on things. Though it wasn't enough to stop the festival altogether.

The residents of Boohail could be in the middle of a raging tsunami and still find an excuse to party. In the distance, I could hear Carter and Katie blaring their latest song for all to hear. The only thing that the couple loved more than their bakery was playing music. A gift they shared any chance they could. Not to be outdone, most of the shop owners in the village had set up stalls lining Boohail's center. Bright banners and shimmering lanterns lit up our small corner of the world like a sea of stars. Delicious smells of festival food and incense greeted you everywhere you turned. Even with everything that's changed in the short amount of time, a party just made everything feel like home.

Priscilla did her best to help Cin explain to the rest of Boohail that her new friends meant no harm and it was, in fact, our own goddess causing all demons to become crazed animals. But some villagers took it better than others. Humans had been worshiping the goddess Myva for hundreds of years. To find out it had all been a lie crafted by some undead witch was hard to swallow.

A small faction of men, in particular, attempted to form a mob and kill as many of the newcomers as possible. That idea was firmly put to bed when Fallon turned into a giant dragon. The fiery smoke around his mouth was enough to get even the most zealous men to drop their weapons. If I remembered correctly, Jack was one of them. Gods, the money I would have paid to see that smug asshole piss himself at the sight.

Jack smiled, combing a hand through his dark curls. "OK, no need to bite my head off. I'll go fix you a drink, Brie. Maybe it will loosen you up. You seem tense."

This fucking guy.

My response spat out through gritted teeth. "I'm not tense. I'm annoyed that you keep bothering me. This—" my finger waved in between us "—will not happen."

"Sure, sure," he replied before turning and walking away.

My shoulders slumped. It was like talking to a sleeping hog. I made my way over to a food stall and placed an order for two more baked potatoes. Once the vendor quickly wrapped up the steaming treats, I rejoined Cin and Fallon at the row of bar stools next to the mead stall. My body slumped over the counter and I let out a sigh. Cin reached over to snatch her food before taking a large bite.

Without a word, Sunbeam placed a mug in front of me and went back to washing out more cups. The barmaid was one of the few humans seemingly unfazed by Boohail's newest residents. Though it didn't seem like anything fazed her. Ever. Her bright name was a hilarious contrast to her stern and serious demeanor. I suppose you'd have to be on the sterner side to run a tavern on your own. The large-and-in-charge woman was famous for her no-nonsense attitude toward sloppy drunks. Anyone who posed a threat to destroying any bit of her precious tavern was thrown out without remorse. My hand snaked around the handle of my drink before downing half. The sweet taste of honey and peach washed over me, taking away most of my irritation.

"My friend has a hyena we could feed him to," Cin said, patting my back. She laughed at my concerned look and took another bite of her potato. "I'm just saying we have options!"

"You're a lot more bloodthirsty than I remember."

She held up a finger to give herself time to chew. "Killing a goddess will do that to ya."

"I…can't argue with that." The rest of my drink found its way down my throat and Sunbeam reached over to refill the mug. Her lips formed a thin line as she glanced at my side. A large red hand slammed on the counter, making me jump.

"Sunbeam, my precious day bringer! Have you missed me?" An orc the size of a bear sat on the stool next to me. The newcomer hunched his large body over the counter and rested his chin on his hands.

His eyes blatantly roved over Sunbeam before he broke out into a goofy grin. The woman in question only gave him an impassive stare. Her tone was the definition of ice. "What will it be, Balabash?"

The red orc grinned wider. Thick tusks poked out the sides of his lower jaw, giving the large man an even more menacing appearance. "How about a kiss from my honey butter biscuit?"

Fallon spat out his drink and choked on a laugh. His wife snickered and patted his back. Of all the lame pickup lines I've ever heard, that may have taken the cake.

To my surprise, Sunbeam's stoic face gave way to a mortified sputter. Quickly, she turned her back to him and snatched a bottle from the lower shelf of her stand. "Just for that, you get the weak brew!"

The bottle slammed down in front of Balabash, whose face remained as gleeful as ever. He took the bottle with a wink, which Sunbeam returned by marching away from him and busying herself by ferociously scrubbing the glass she just cleaned.

Balabash took a swig from the bottle and leaned down to

whisper in my ear. "She wants me." I covered my mouth to stifle a laugh. That may have been the first time I'd seen any emotion on the woman's face.

"Bash, she'll kill you at this rate," Cinnamon warned.

He waved her off and took another swig. "Nonsense! My Sunbeam is just a little shy, is all." He caught sight of his "precious day bringer" glaring at him from across the bar. She ducked her head back down to the innocent glass she was mauling and scrubbed harder. "Don't worry, my love, I am a patient man!"

"Oh, just take your bottle and go!" she snapped. My eyes widened at the high pitch in her voice.

Oh, this is just delicious. The stoic barmaid and flirtatious orc. I'd read that romance novel any day. With any luck, I'd be able to find more monster romance books in the coming years. Now that more humans could interact with them, it was only a matter of time that my favorite authors graced me with saucy tales of their new source material.

"Whatever you say, man," Cin said. "Anyway, this is my bestie, Brie. Brie, this is Balabash. He worked in the kitchens with me on the ship."

Balabash turned in his seat to tower over—I mean, face me. My polite nod was met with another wide grin before a bear paw of a hand crashed down on my shoulder, nearly knocking me off my chair. "Good to meet you, Miss Brie! Any friend of Cin's is a friend of mine!"

7

Before I could answer, my self-appointed friend spun me around on my stool to face Cin. The orc's free hand crashed down on my other shoulder as my life flashed before my eyes. I never expected to meet my end by an overly enthusiastic orc greeting, but life was an unpredictable bitch.

"What do you mean by best friend, though?" Balabash asked, giving my shoulders a little shake. "I thought Felix was your best friend. You're not two-timing my little brother, are you?"

Cinnamon rolled her eyes. "Don't be so dramatic. Brie is my best friend and Felix is my best demon friend. Don't worry, you're on the list too," she said, waving him off. "Friendship is a level, not a straight line."

Balabash pulled me back and leaned in to whisper in my ear. The food and booze in my gut rolled in protest with each new movement. "Can you believe this? She's cheating on us with each other."

"I'm gonna puke if you don't stop whipping me around, friend."

"Yes, I think it's about time you got your hands off her." Jack's voice and the jostled contents of my stomach were way too annoying to deal with at the same time.

Ignoring Jack, Balabash released my shoulders. "Sorry Brie, I forget humans are less sturdy than my kind." His large hands gave a small pat to smooth out my ruffled blouse before he turned back to the bar. "Sunbeam, could you bring me another of whatever my new friend is having?"

I could feel the scowl on Jack's face without even having to turn around. "That won't be necessary," he snapped. "I've bought Brie another drink."

That hyena plan sounds better and better every time he opens his mouth. I wouldn't call Jack particularly ugly. He may have even passed for handsome if he wasn't so blindly annoying and easy to see through. The whole town knew of Jack's ambitious nature and his inability to budget. It wouldn't surprise me in the slightest if creditors were knocking at his door once again.

Last I heard, his latest get-rich-quick scheme involved buying expensive fancy chickens that lay black eggs and trying to sell them on the market for twice the price of a normal egg. The only problem was that no one in Boohail cared about what color a fucking egg was. I could see the idea working if we lived near some posh city with easily amused rich people. But the closest thing we had to rich folk was Cin's family, the Hotpeppers. I practically grew up in Cin's home and she and her family never once turned to me and said, "You know what would make this omelet better? If it was just straight black."

He probably looked at me and saw a cash cow more than a wife. If my land wasn't directly next to his, I doubt he'd ever give me the time of day. My neighbor was a pushy nuisance with his eye on expansion, and I'd have to be an idiot not to see it. We've lived our whole lives in Boohail and yet he never deemed me worthy to speak to until I bought my small plot of land off Cinnamon's family. Then suddenly I was the apple of his eye. And I was getting very sick of it.

My face hardened, and I turned to look him dead in the eye. "Jack, I've told you once, I've told you a thousand times. I am not interested. I do not want your drink. Leave me alone."

The smile never left his face as he pushed a fizzing pink drink into my hands. "Don't be like that, sweetheart! Just try it. It's a special cocktail I made just for you!"

Fighting back my anger, I grit my teeth and pushed the drink back into his hands. "I don't want it."

A small crack appeared in the man's smile. "Just try it," he said, pushing it back.

"No."

"For me?"

"Extra no."

His smile finally dropped to a sneer. "Don't be so stubborn!" He pushed the drink back into my hands.

Unable to see through the haze of my anger, I snatched the cup back and finally snapped. "For the last damn time, I DON'T WANT YOUR DRINK." With the force of every woman tired of broke men's audacity, I yeeted the drink straight at Jack's head. Unfortunately for me, that broke man could dodge.

I watched in horror as Jack ducked down, letting the fizzing pink drink fly straight over his head to crash into a mess of blond hair. My unsuspecting victim flinched, rubbing the back of his head before whipping around with a glare.

Time seemed to slow at that moment. My breath caught; icy blue eyes rooted me to my chair. The man straightened, revealing a tall, muscled frame. His wavy blond hair framed high cheekbones and a face that could lead a woman to sin. I watched on, entranced, as his eyes widened. The blue sea receded against the black abyss of his pupils. His mouth dropped open as if he was seeing something unimaginable, like a boa constrictor getting up and walking away.

"Look, I'm sorry about that," I mumbled. "I didn't mean to hit you. Does your head hurt?" My hand skimmed the bar, trying to find a cloth to help wipe him off. But when I turned back around, the stranger was on me. A firm arm slid around my back, his free hand cupped my chin, tilting my face to his before capturing my lips in a kiss. His eager mouth muffled my small squeak. My knees grew weak when the stranger nipped my lower lip, taking the chance to deepen the kiss further when my lips parted in shock. I tried to signal my hands to push him off. But the treacherous heathens only rested on a broad chest.

A rush of cold hit me and I opened my eyes to see the bold stranger had been yanked back by Jack. He fisted the blond man's collar before yelling obscenities in his ear. But the stranger barely took notice of him. He shook his head, as if trying to clear his thoughts, before shoving Jack to the side. In a flash, his hands were on me again. This time cupping my face to look me over, disbelief and wonder shining through his smiling face.

"Felix?" Cin's voice was careful and measured. "You OK, bud? You're coming on a little strong to my friend there."

Her voice shook him out of whatever trance he was in. He chuckled before smiling, his face lighting up like Sunbeam's namesake. "I'm better than OK," he said, tracing the outline of my jaw with the back of his knuckles. "I just imprinted on my mate."

I reeled, hitting my lower back against the bar. "What!?" Cin and I screamed in unison.

To my side, Balabash cheered, and Fallon pounded a fist on the bar. "Sunbeam, we're going to need shots over here. Keep them coming, please!" The dragon shifter and the orc rose from their seats to clap Felix on the back and congratulated us on a happy life.

Felix reached for me again, but I put a hand on his face and shoved him away. Or tried to. A slight struggle ensued in which I continued pushing on his face and he insistently tried to collect me into his arms again. I looked at Cin, but she simply sat there, mouth open and eyes wide. No help at all. "You want to slow down and maybe tell me what the hell's going on here?"

He leaned back, placing his hands on my knees, giving me a temporary reprieve from our struggle. "I'm sorry dear, I forgot you're human." His voice maintained a chipper note, as if this was the most delightful occasion to ever occur. "You see, when my kind sees their mate for the first time, we know instantly. Which is known as an imprint. For me, that's you."

He took my hand and kissed my knuckles. The gesture sent a small thrill up my spine.

I blinked. "And what exactly is your kind?"

"Hold on," Cin piped up. "Jack, what's that bottle you just dropped?"

The man on the floor turned pale. He scrambled to pick up the bottle, but Fallon beat him to it. In a last-ditch effort, Jack took a swipe at the demon's arm, but Fallon merely swatted him off. The bottle held a small pinch of glittering pink liquid as he held it up to his face. Fallon turned to view the back of it, where I could make out a bright blue label. His mouth formed a thin line and let out an irritated growl. "It's a love potion."

Without thinking, I snatched one shot off the counter and threw it back. Its sweet tang was a much-needed comfort, and I knew without a shadow of a doubt that I would need a lot more of them before the night was over. "How do you know it's a love potion?"

"It says so right on the bottle." Fallon handed me the potion and motioned to Balabash. The orc nodded and stepped on Jack, who was attempting to crawl away. The farmer's chest met the cobblestone street with an ungraceful thump.

I glanced at Felix, but he held the same dopey smile. Either he wasn't paying attention or he simply didn't care. Instead, he took the opportunity to nuzzle my neck once the hand pushing him away was occupied. His breath came out as a warm sigh against my collarbone. The chilly air of a crisp fall afternoon was chased away by his large body pressing closer to mine. Bolder still, Felix rested his chin against my shoulder and wrapped his arms around the small of my back.

Oddly enough, I didn't feel the need to punch him in the face. Physical touch wasn't something I particularly enjoyed. Looking back, I could think of at least one or two instances where my aversion to physical affection caused a rift between a lover or a friend. I doubted any of the Hotpeppers had hugged me more than once. Much to my surrogate ma's dismay. Yet instead of the skin-crawling sensation I'd come to expect, Felix's intrusion into my personal space didn't set me off at all. If anything, I just wanted another shot.

As if reading my thoughts, Cin passed another of the perfectly polished glasses my way and nodded at the potion. *Bless her soul.* Ignoring the needy demon in my lap, I focused my attention on the half-empty glass. The words "LOVE POTION" were spelled out in bright gold letters across the front. On the back, in a much smaller font, were instructions. I downed my second shot before reading them aloud.

"Apply six ounces of Love Potion directly onto or into the desired person's drink. Make sure you stand directly in front of the user, as they will fall madly in love with the first person they see once the potion takes hold. Reapply every two weeks for maintained effect. Warning: do not use if you are pregnant or think you may become pregnant. Side effects may include itching, obsessive behavior, impulsiveness and aggression, panic attacks, and in severe cases, a loss of consciousness and heart failure."

My body felt cold once the gravity of the situation fell on me. *That piece of shit tried to drug me.*

From the ground, Jack let out a choked gasp under the weight of Balabash's foot. Which was still planted firmly on his back. The look of that slimy rat on the ground filled me with more hatred than I knew I was capable of. His eyes met mine, and I could just see him trying to form a new scheme in his head. Some way to deflect the situation where he could still come out on top and get what he wanted. I held his gaze and dropped the bottle. "Crush him."

Jack squeaked and tried to squirm his way from under the orc. But Balabash needed no further invitation and put even more pressure on the man's back. "Brie wait, it's not what it looks like!"

The red orc grunted and lifted the squirming rat from the floor. "I've heard enough, tiny man." Balabash turned to give me a bright smile. "Don't worry Brie, we'll take care of this problem for you. He won't bother you again."

To my side, Fallon cracked his knuckles and glanced at his wife. Cin inspected her nails before swirling the mead cup in her hand. "Just don't kill him, love. We don't need the villagers to be even more scared of you than they already are."

His returning grin held a sadistic glint that would have given me goosebumps under normal circumstances. But as it stood, the gesture warmed my enraged heart. Jack wouldn't weasel his way out of that asswhooping.

Balabash clamped his hand around Jack's mouth, and Fallon threw an arm around the doomed man as if they were old friends. With a wave, the two demons escorted the squirming man away from the stall and into the crowd of other festival-goers. A young couple turned to look at the odd trio as they left, but Katie immediately stole their attention, dropping to her knees in a flute solo.

Cin let out a deep sigh and took a generous sip of her drink. "Well, that's taken care of. What do we do about him?" she said, pointing to the man still wrapped around my waist.

"Great question." Thanks to my earlier stunt, Felix took the full brunt of the love potion. If his clingy behavior was any indication, the potion worked as advertised. "Um, Felix?"

The blond lifted his head and brushed a curl out of my face. "Yes, love?"

"Oh, boy." His look of hopeful reverence gave me the sinking feeling that I was about to kick a puppy. Not a great night for me. "So, not sure if you heard," I began slowly. "But it looks like a love potion has struck you. I'm sorry, but I'm not your mate."

"I disagree," he said simply.

"Sorry, did you miss the part about the love potion?"

"Yes, beloved, I can hear just fine. I just disagree."

Behind me, Sunbeam tsked and set another shot on the table. My hand slid to snatch it up as if on instinct. "Why do you disagree? The proof is right on the bottle."

Felix caught my hand holding the shot glass. My body tensed with a sudden awareness as he leaned in. The warm scent of sandalwood drifted past my nose as I felt the barest whisper against my ear. "Love potion or not, you can't fake a hunger like this. If it weren't for this crowd, I'd show you just how much I already burn for you. You're mine, Brie."

A lump formed in my throat and I tried to stomp down the shiver threatening to give away just how much I'd taken notice of him. He winked at me before lifting my hand to his lips and downing my shot.

The chill of the night broke through when he finally pulled away. "I need to deal with the man who thought to take you from me. So I'll leave you for tonight, sweetheart." With that, Felix turned and walked away.

I stared at my hand. The soft feeling of his lips against my fingers left a shadowed sensation I wasn't sure how to respond to. Beside me, Cin sat wide-eyed, sipping her drink. After a slight pause, she lowered her cup and shook her head in pity. "You are *so* fucked."

"Yeah, that's not helping." My hand found another shot, and I threw it back.

She chuckled and waved her hand dismissively. "You'll be fine. Felix is a sweetheart."

"A drugged sweetheart," Sunbeam muttered as she sat down another round of drinks.

"Exactly, Sunbeam gets it," I shouted, pointing to the bartender.

Cinnamon rolled her eyes. "Do you just wanna wait here until the fellas get back? I could mediate a chat for you two so you can discuss what to do about this love potion situation."

It wasn't a poor plan for sure. Yet the thought of more social interaction made me want to crawl into a hole for at least a week. "I think I've had enough for today. Lemme sleep this off and I'd be happy to meet up and get things sorted tomorrow."

I paid my tab, lit my lantern and bid the two goodnight. I had no intention of accidentally running into more of my new friends, so I veered off Boohail's main road and headed into a smaller path behind the market stalls I often used for deliveries.

The roar of the festival crowd died down into peaceful silence. Cool night air brushed pleasantly past my shot-warmed cheeks. "What a night," I said to myself. When the world was quiet enough for me to hear my own thoughts, I let my mind drift to Felix's earlier words.

"When my kind sees their mate for the first time, we know instantly."

I wondered what his kind was. He didn't have horns like Fallon, so he probably wasn't a dragon. Thank the stars. To his credit, the man had been nothing but polite since Cin brought him home, but I still haven't forgotten the way he almost ripped a man's arm off in front of me.

In the distance, a sharp scream erupted from the trees. Startled, I tripped over myself and looked around. "What the fuck was that?" I rasped. The silent woods around me gave no answers. Taking deep breaths, I continued walking.

"Maybe it was just a puma that has come down from the mountains." Pumas made the most terrifying noises. Every time one of those overgrown cats came close to the village, we'd be stuck with a sea of screeching caterwauling until the damn thing moved on. "Yeah, it's just another damn puma."

A soft voice called out from the trees. "Hello."

Pausing, I stopped and looked toward the noise. "Yeah?" I answered.

"Hello," the voice called again.

"Yes, hello what's up?" I couldn't see who was calling. But they didn't sound far away. I wondered briefly if some drunk idiot fell off the trail and got stuck in a prickle bush. Not that I was one to judge. We've all drunkenly tripped and gotten stuck in a barrel or two at some point in our lives.

"Hello."

Annoyed, I spoke a little louder. "Yes, hello, we've established greetings. What do you need? Are you stuck?"

"Hello."

"Well, fuck you then," I said, swatting at the voice. "I'm too tired for this level of patience." Stomping away, I ignored the repetitive twat and kept moving. Whoever it was fell quiet. I sighed in relief at not having to deal with any other social interactions. No more people for tonight, thank you.

Something moved impossibly fast in the trees and stopped a little way behind me. "Hello."

I clicked my tongue, nodding as a rush of fear traveled down my spine. "Yup. That's a damn demon." Not bothering to look back, I hauled ass down the road toward my farm.

Sharp ticks of claws against stone met my ears, followed by a low hiss. I peeked over my shoulder. The creature darting after me was an immense mass of slithering grass-like hair. It had the arms and legs of a human but crawled on all fours with the swaying gait of an alligator. Its long jaw opened wide, showing off rows of serrated, sharp teeth. I screamed and pushed my legs faster, cursing my mother, father, and all my ancestors for my stubby legs.

The beast closed the distance between us, snapping at the hem of my skirt. I shrieked and swung my lantern at it. It hissed angrily and slowed down, only to regain its composure and dart after me again. Its clawed hand shot out and seized my ankle, sending me to the ground.

"Get off me," I cried out, kicking at the offending hand. I grabbed a handful of dirt, but when I turned to throw it in the creature's eyes, something had ripped it off of me. The alligator freak let off a pained cry.

Moonlight flickered through the trees, revealing my savior. Unfortunately for my unlucky ass, that savior was an even bigger monster. The newcomer snarled, tearing into the flesh of the gator beast like it was parchment paper. It was too dim to make out the exact features of the beast. All I could tell was that, unlike the gator, this one stood on two legs. Its body was covered in light-colored fur and was clearly twice as pissed off as the smaller monster it was mauling.

The gator shrieked and the sound of snapping bones cut through the air. I cried out when something landed in front of me. I held the lantern up, then held down vomit when the light flickered against a severed arm.

Scrambling to my feet, I took off running. Hoping the gator monster was enough to sate the appetite of whatever the hell that thing was.

"Brie, stop." A loud thud hit the ground.

I turned to see the light-colored beast had tossed aside the gator monster to chase after me. Fear-soaked tears blurred my vision. "Get away from me. I don't taste good," I screamed.

The beast let out a low rumble and ran faster. "I'm not going to eat you. Just stop." In a flash, the demon darted in front of me and grabbed my shoulders when I slammed into its chest.

Panic made my breath come out in jumbled gasps. A wave of dizziness went through my mind until my knees buckled. The monstrous hands kept a firm grip on my shoulders as they led me gently to the ground. "You're hyperventilating. Just focus on breathing for me."

Claws gripped my chin and forced me to look up into glowing, blood-red eyes. My vision swam and everything went dark.

Chapter 2

Brie

A pox on whatever fool felt the need to rummage around my kitchen. I turned over in my bed, trying to block out the occasional bump and clatter of pans coming from the room below. The darkness beyond my window gave testament to the fact that whoever was down there, a robber, a friend coming for fresh cheese, or any sort of drunkard, was here way too fucking early.

My head was killing me. I still had on the blouse and skirt I wore the day before, and they were covered in sweat and dirt. My idiot self must have stumbled home after too many shots. Flashes of monsters chasing me through the woods had me rubbing my temples in frustration. Nightmares were the worst.

Another loud clang caused me to flinch and burrow further under my many fluffy blankets. Not only was that prick too early, but they had no regard for the concept of a hangover. If they had come here just to steal the prized Gouda I had stored in my pantry, then they should have just taken it and fucking left. Briefly, I wondered if it was the same teenager that broke into my family's cheese shop the week prior. Yet another stupid dare made by teenage idiots that always seem to cost more to those around them than the troublemakers themselves.

The intruder made a low rumbling noise, followed by the sound of more shuffling. Things quieted for a moment and I went back to my task of ignoring it.

Another bang.

"Fuck," a deep voice cursed.

I sighed and threw the covers off me. Dim morning light illuminated my bedroom in a soft glow. The gentle blue pastels of its interior did nothing to soothe my raging headache. If there is any justice in this world, I would have been allowed to sleep the day away and pretend the world didn't exist until tomorrow. But peace would not be found until whatever asshole that was downstairs met my wrath.

Absently, I tucked my titties back into my breast band after their daring escape in the night, then changed my muddy clothes for a halfway presentable nightgown and threw on a bonnet to hide my wild hair. I donned a pair of slippers and snatched a long knitting needle off the nightstand. The cool weight of the metal in my hand felt comforting in its familiarity. The dull thing wouldn't be much use if I actually had to use it, and I was more used to stabbing through a difficult coat pattern than an annoying intruder, but I assumed the threat of the long needle would get the job done. As soon as they had been scared off, my Blanket Kingdom would once again welcome me with open arms.

Not bothering to tiptoe around my own house, I stomped my way into the kitchen. Brandishing the needle like a dagger, I kicked open my kitchen door. "What's a woman gotta do to get some goddamn sle—"

My words cut off and my body froze up. It took a moment for my mind to even process what it was seeing. I held on to the door frame to keep myself upright after my knees threatened to give out. *Maybe the shots I had last night were spiked?* Yes, that made sense. It would explain the weird nightmare as well. The monster that stood next to my fireplace was just some drug-fueled joke gone wrong.

Yet when I shook my head to clear my mind, the beast was still there. It stood on two legs, the top of its head nearly reaching the ceiling. Its massive body was covered in shaggy fur the color of fresh corn. The beast stiffened, finally taking notice of my presence. My heart hammered in my chest as I watched the creature slowly turn around. The red eyes of a massive wolflike creature locked on to my trembling frame, sending icy fear down my spine. Stranger still, the beast had on my apron. The frilly green garment was strained over the monster wolf's torso, making the smiley face I had sewn on stretch into a worried thin grimace.

"What…what the fuck?"

Turning fully to face me, the beast set down a wooden bowl on the counter. "Brie." My name came out in a rumble past vicious-looking fangs. Every instinct in my body screamed for self-preservation, and I agreed wholeheartedly. However, the rest of my body was a tad slower than my feet. The needle fell from my hand and skittered underneath my kitchen table as I crashed to the floor like a sack of potatoes. Without bothering to look back, I scrambled up and bolted through my front door. I could hear the scrape of claws against hardwood floors behind me and it only spurred me faster while I ran screaming towards my barn.

"Brie wait!"

Sweet melted fontina, it wasn't a dream!

Sheep scattered out of the way. I knocked a bale of hay over in an attempt to slow my attacker and rushed toward the large red door of the barn. The monster jumped over the fallen hay as if it were nothing and closed the distance between us. I screamed and hit the door with a thud, then forced it open and scrambled inside. Before I could slam it shut, the beast slammed a clawed hand on the door. I let out another shriek and stumbled back.

The creature braced his other hand on the door frame, his breath coming out in deep, slow pants. With a grunt, the wooden door was slammed open, its hinges creaking with the excessive display of force. His chest gave another shuddering exhale before his gaze lifted to pin me in place. Dagger-like teeth flashed into a hungry grin that seemed oddly familiar. "Please don't run from me, Brie," he panted. "It's getting me a little too excited."

Goosebumps raced down my arms. The predator in the doorway set off every alarm bell in my soul, but the way he said my name gnawed at me. I swallowed spit and tried to find my voice. "Felix?"

The beast grinned wider. "Good morning."

I licked my lips and tried to convince my heart to stop trying to beat its way out of my chest. "What are you doing here?"

His enormous wolf's ears perked up, and he pointed a thumb back toward the house. "I'm making you breakfast." How he managed to sound guttural, fierce, and chipper at the same time was beyond me.

I nodded once. "OK...how did you get into my house?"

The question caused his grin to finally fade. The werewolf scratched the back of his head and shifted his eyes away. "Um...do you not remember fainting last night? I didn't want you to have to sleep outside, so I carried you to your bed."

The memory of the two terrifying creatures became clearer

in my mind. "Right...so that was real. Did you find out where I hid my spare key then? I don't recall taking one with me." I always lost the damn thing whenever I went out. So I just kept a spare hidden in the wind chime on my porch.

Felix refused to look up from a nail on the floor. "Well, no. I didn't see a key anywhere."

My eyes narrowed. "Did I leave my kitchen window open?"

He glanced at me nervously, then shifted his gaze back to the floor. "No, I used the front door. It just...needed a little push."

"You broke my door?"

"I can fix it," he said quickly, shifting his weight back and forth.

I guess I should just be happy he took me home instead of eating me. But why was he still here?

"I wanted to apologize for scaring you last night, so I did a few chores around your home since I was already here. After I fixed the fence, milked the goats, and let the animals out to pasture, I wasn't sure what else you took care of in the morning. I bathed a few of the sheep, but that black one is an ornery beast and I had to shift just to get him to heel."

The werewolf paced in the doorway as he continued to ramble off chores and menial tasks. My head spun, and I looked around the barn to see that he had in fact filled up the milk jugs and even swept out each stall. I held a hand up and he silenced himself. "Felix," I began slowly. "Where did you sleep?"

A long tail twitched behind him. "I didn't."

I rubbed my temples in an attempt to soothe the still raging headache. "How did you even know where I live?"

"I'm a werewolf, Lamb. I followed your scent."

My head fell to my knees. "Snapping gators."

"Please don't be mad," Felix whispered. "I didn't intend to stay once I put you in bed, but the harder I tried to leave, the more frantic I became. I know humans don't imprint like we do, so I wanted to give you space. But every second I wasn't near, you tore at me. Finding tasks to do around your house was the only thing keeping me from barging into your bedroom."

He stumbled back at my stunned look, holding his arms up in a placating manner. "Not that I would force anything!" he shouted. "Gods no. I just…"

The werewolf sighed and sat down in the doorway. His large head hung low as he pinched the bridge of his nose. Snout. Whatever.

After a moment, he let off an irritated growl. His gaze searched mine as if I had the answers to his wild behavior. "I'm usually a lot smoother than this. I swear."

Maybe it was the absurdity of the situation or my lack of sleep, but I just started laughing and found it difficult to stop. Felix looked up at me with a hopeful expression, his tail losing some of that nervous twitch. When I tried to compose myself long enough to look him in the eye, the werewolf dropped his ears like a sad dog waiting to be chastised, and I just laughed even harder.

"Would breakfast help my case at all?" he asked.

I wiped a tear from my eye and sat up straighter. "Is that what's burning?"

Felix shot up in a panic. "Oh fuck, my eggs!" The werewolf ran back to the house, scaring the poor sheep once more. A chorus of banging pans followed not far behind.

It was then I noticed Kevin, my black ram. His normally coarse coat shone like black diamonds in the sunlight. He stomped his hoof and threw his impressive horns in Felix's direction, as if to tell the world just how pissed off he was at the impromptu grooming. At the base of his left horn was a tattered piece of brown cloth. No doubt a remnant of the fight he must have put up.

Even I had a hard time getting that bully to do anything without getting a hoof to the chest. If he didn't give off such fine wool, I would have turned him into mutton chops years ago. Little shit.

I made my way back into the kitchen to see an increasingly distraught werewolf trying to beat smoke out of the small window above the counter. His massive frame was still deeply intimidating, but from what I could tell, he meant no harm.

Deep breaths, Brie.

"Felix, why don't you go have a seat in the other room?"

The demon began to make a noise of protest, but hushed

when I grabbed his arm and gently but firmly pulled him out of the kitchen. In his werewolf form, he could have easily shaken me off, but instead he closed his free hand over the one I had on his arm and let himself be led out of the smoking room. I motioned for him to sit down on a plush love seat and kicked a footstool near his feet. "Just wait here a bit and I'll bring us some coffee and a snack."

Felix moved to stand back up. "Brie, wait, let me help."

"Sit," I ordered without turning back.

A few minutes and a smoke-free kitchen later, I returned with fresh coffee and a plate of grilled cheese sandwiches. Not the fanciest breakfast, but it got the job done in a pinch. Cooking wasn't normally something I enjoyed, anyway. So the simple dish had its merits, in my opinion.

"OK, so I hope you like—WHERE ARE YOUR CLOTHES?"

In my brief absence, Felix had returned to his human form. His very naked human form. He still wore my frilly green apron, but nothing else. A beautiful sight that happily burrowed its way into my mind, never to leave again. I probably should have turned away, but considering all that happened that morning, a well-muscled chest seemed like a fair payment. He interrupted my sleep, after all. The sight of all that smooth, fair skin pulled over the tight cords of his muscles was definitely worth waking up for.

Felix's face blushed scarlet and quickly tugged at the pants around his ankles. "Sorry," he murmured. "My clothes don't transform with me. So I took them off while I was working outside." He must have noticed my appreciative glance, and paused his movements.

Was I drooling? No. No dammit, I'm a lady.

Felix raised a brow. "Or I could keep them off if this is working for you?"

"No!" I snapped, placing the food and drinks on my coffee table. "Put your clothes back on."

He hummed and did as instructed. But not without a satisfied grin the whole way through.

Once dressed, Felix took his place back on the love seat. I slumped down in the armchair across from him and sighed at the soothing scent of morning coffee. The cheesy goodness of the first bite of my sandwich made the morning better all around. Logically, I felt I should be more concerned at the fact that I was sitting across from the man that broke into my home, but I felt partially responsible for his behavior. What with yeeting a love potion at his head and all. If the warning on the side of the bottle was true, then crazy erratic behavior would be something I'd have to deal with for the next couple of weeks. Honestly, a man showing up and doing my chores wasn't the worst thing to happen to a woman.

"Obviously, we need to talk about what happened last night," I began after a sip of coffee.

Running a hand through his blond hair, the man leaned back in the love seat as if he owned it. "I just feel like I'd hear you a lot better if you were over here next to me. My senses are dulled in this form, you know." He patted his lap in invitation.

"Don't push your luck."

"Damn." Whether the immediate rejection affected him didn't show on his face. The same easygoing smile remained through his cup of coffee.

I polished off my grilled cheese and was hounding for another, but polite society demanded I wait until my guest took his first. "Please, help yourself to a few sandwiches."

Felix glanced at the plate in front of us. Four ticks of the clock went by. "Do you not like grilled cheese? I can try to whip up something else."

"No. No, this is fine."

Judging by the twitch at the edge of his grin, logic would determine that was a lie.

Sitting up straighter in his seat, Felix took hold of the top sandwich. A string of sharp cheddar stretched its steaming goodness against the one below before breaking off. The man stared long and hard at the treat before taking a large bite out of the corner. "So, what did you want to discuss?"

Well, for starters, why are you being so weird about a sandwich?

"Judging by what I read off the back of that love potion, it looks like you're going to be stuck like this for at least two weeks. We should make a few ground rules on how to handle the situation until you go back to normal."

"This is my normal now, beloved. I've imprinted on you."

He finished off his sandwich with grim determination and eased back in his seat.

"You don't know that for sure, though. It could just be the love potion affecting you."

"How many kids do you want?"

I choked on my coffee. Spilling the hot liquid over the front of my nightgown. The werewolf calmly walked to the closet next to my bookshelf, took out a neatly folded hand towel, and handed it to me. Never in the half hour that I'd been aware of his presence did I show him where I kept the towels. *How long has he been in here?*

"Come again?" I asked, coughing.

Relaxing back into the love seat, Felix waved a hand around the room. "Kids. Your home is cozy, but small. If we're going to have more than two, then I'll need to build an extension. If we knock out the back wall in your sewing room, that would be a fine place for it."

"Hold on!"

Blue eyes took on a wistful note as he continued. "A huge family has been a dream of mine, so I'm partial to ten, but I'm willing to negotiate."

Choking turned into harsh wheezing. The risk of suffocation grew each second I couldn't figure out how to get that damn coffee down my throat. Felix moved to sit on the armrest of my chair and rubbed circles along my back. "Easy darling, take small breaths."

Ten kids. My mind was reeling. I barely saw my ma and my brother Gouda more than once a week if it could be avoided. We'd gotten our family cheese shop down to a strict pattern where I made the cheese and dropped it off, Gouda sold the cheese, and our mom was off somewhere in the abyss, leaving us the hell alone. None of us were much in the way of affection and liked to keep it that way. Spending time at Cin's home growing up gave me a small insight into what a normal family might look like. But even before her sister, Cherry, disappeared, there were only six of them! More importantly, I could leave when it got too rowdy for my liking. Having ten kids running around my quiet home sounded like a punishment for past life grievances.

"Slow down," I snapped, getting up. "There's no reason to even talk about that now. You'll forget about this whole thing once the love potion wears off."

"Or it won't." His tone dropped to something low and dangerous. I found myself backed into my bookshelf as he grew closer. Felix braced an arm above my head and gently traced my jawline with the back of his knuckles. Once again, my heart felt it pertinent to form an escape plan and renewed its efforts to beat out of my chest. "Is it really so hard to believe that you're mine? I've been under the effect of my fair share of spells. Nothing has affected me with this much…intensity." Soft lips grazed the skin just above my ear. I shivered as his hand eased its way down my body to settle on my waist.

Words... how speak? "Umm," came my eloquent response.

"Is it the thought of a fated mate that scares you?" His deep voice caressed my ear in a way that reminded me of just how deeply single I'd been the past year. "Judging by the rather interesting books you have on this shelf, I assumed the idea might excite you."

Oh gods, he found my romance books.

His mouth curved in a smile against my temple. "Let's see, 'Wicked Wolves and Wandering Women,' 'A Shifter's Desires.'"

Kill me now.

My tormentor paused for a moment, then removed his hand to snatch a book from the shelf. " 'Rejected By Her Alpha Mate: Rejected Princess Book 01'?"

My stomach bottomed out. *Anything but that series!* "Rejected Princess" was one of the craziest series I'd ever gotten into. The plot lines were filled with ridiculous angst, cheesy lines about true love and sex, and made a point to shove in every possible trope it could. But damn if I didn't eat up that fifteen-book series like it was my job.

"Now why in the world would anyone reject their mate?"

I shot a hand out to grab it back, but the tall bastard easily raised it out of my reach. "Look, that series came out years ago. It was a different time in the romance game!"

Ignoring my retrieval attempts, Felix read the first few pages and tutted. "Even if Darren is in love with Jolene, you can't fight an imprint. They should just bid each other farewell and be done with it."

He easily dodged another swipe at the book. "It's not that simple!" I huffed. "Jolene threatens to banish Dolly to The Realm of Forgotten Women, if Darren doesn't agree to marry her. It's a layered plot, OK?"

Felix snickered and held the book higher. "I see. Nothing wrong with a bit of drama in a love story. Judging by the sea of Alpha titles and barrel-chested men on the covers, is it fair to say an aggressive approach would work better on you?"

A shiver ran down my spine at the predatory glint in his eyes. Felix slammed his free hand on the shelf behind me, just to the side of my head, boxing me in. He leaned in close until his breath whispered against my face. "Should I growl in your ear that you're mine and toss you over my shoulder? I admit it's not my style, but for you, Lamb? Anything."

This man was a menace to my heart.

It wasn't as if I was ashamed of my reading choices, but having a shelf full of werewolf love stories was a little awkward when I had an actual werewolf backing me against them. Despite the indignation, I couldn't help but squeeze my thighs together as heat pooled in between them. Naughty fantasies I'd normally reserved for my nights alone came racing to mind.

The deep blue of his eyes darkened into something

reminiscent of storming seas. He leaned closer still and licked his lips. An action that had no right to be that enticing. When I turned away, he placed the book back on the shelf and lifted my chin, forcing me to look at him. "Just say the word, Lamb. Tell me you want me too. I'd be more than happy to fulfill any desires those books gave you."

My breath came out in a harsh shudder and I closed my eyes to will away poor decisions. "I can't."

His thumb stroked my jawline in a slow, gentle rhythm. "Why?"

I blinked and tried to refocus my thoughts. "It wouldn't be right. You're drugged, and I don't want you to do something you'll regret."

Felix chuckled, a small dimple appearing on the left side of his mouth. "A sweet little lamb protecting the virtue of the wolf trying to eat her up. You really are something, Brie. What about when my two weeks are up? If I still burn for you then, what will you do?"

Leaning my head against the shelf, I sighed and let honesty slip through. "I imagine I'll be begging you to bend me over the nearest surface."

Suddenly, the heat of his body was gone. Felix backed away several steps and turned around, running a frantic hand through his hair.

"Too honest?" I asked.

"I've fought an army of manticores, and the dark magic of

a lich. Both tasks pale in comparison to resisting the urge to shred that gown off you and shoving my tongue down your cunt."

I swallowed and slid down the bookshelf to sit on the floor. I crossed my arms to shield my nipples as they perked through the thin fabric of said nightgown. Under normal circumstances, I doubt anyone would consider the long white garment sexy. Especially not with the dancing sheep embroidered along the hem. Let alone the matching bonnet. But the way Felix looked at me would make any woman weak in the knees. "This is…going to be a long two weeks."

"How did Fallon last a month like this?" he muttered.

Fallon, did Cinnamon hit him with a love potion too? I opened my mouth to question him, but was interrupted by a loud gurgle. The werewolf flinched and put a hand to his stomach. "Are you OK?" I asked.

He turned to me and smiled, waving it off. "It's nothing, I'm fine." Another rumble sounded off.

"Are you sure about that?"

"Yes," he blurted. "Well, I've taken up too much of your time. I'll leave you for now and come back tomorrow to fix your door. Or sooner. To be frank, I'm not sure how long I can stay away from you." His smile faltered as another angry rumble filled the room. "Thank you for the coffee and not… you know, not kicking me out right away." Nodding a goodbye, Felix all but ran out of the house.

Realization dawned as I recalled his adverse reaction to the sandwiches. You didn't spend your life in my profession without recognizing the signs of a stomach Armageddon.

Felix was allergic to cheese.

Chapter 3

Felix

That was disastrous. I'm a giant fucking idiot. It wasn't bad enough that I'd frightened her into fainting, then prowled around her home like a stalker; I'd also managed to disgrace myself in front of her. The only saving factor was that I was able to run for the hills before I destroyed her outhouse. Damn sensitive stomach. Damn cheese and milk in all its evil forms.

I slumped back into my cot, sighing. The customary low crash of waves on the ship's hull did nothing to soothe my fears. My behavior wasn't like a stalker. I was one. Even with her scent still fresh on my nose, it pained me physically not to run straight back to her home. Especially when I thought about that ghoul chasing her. With Myva dead and Volsog's gates destroyed, it wasn't too surprising to see any manner of demons popping up closer to human settlements. Hell, I and my crew mates did.

Not that it made me any less angry. I should have gone back and made sure I shredded the damn ghoul to bits. Those mindless pests were not much of a threat to other demons, but they could easily kill a human. Ideas of sneaking back to her farm "just to check on her" made sleeping through the night impossible. Frustrated, I turned to my side and tried to force myself to sleep.

But the moment my eyes closed, Brie's image burned in my mind and I was back in her living room. Back where the air smelled of coffee and lavender and her. I must have spent hours pacing around her house before I gave in to temptation and broke inside. At first, I'd managed to lie to myself and say it was just a small peek at how she lived. Then, when my feet carried me well past peeking range, it became a matter of her safety. What kind of mate would I be if I didn't check my Lamb's home for intruders (aside from me)? A terrible one. That's what.

Not that it mattered. I'd have told myself any nonsense to justify easing my obsession. Even just a little. So I lied to myself when I admired her collection of skillfully knitted ornaments instead of waiting outside like I should have. I lied to myself when I poured over her book collections instead of looking for intruders. And I lied to myself when I began clanging pots together so she'd wake up and speak to me instead of just making her breakfast. Though burning it wasn't the initial plan. Neither was practically foaming at the mouth anytime she spoke.

"Next time I'll be calm." Probably another lie. But a man could hope. Next time...I want to see the way her nose scrunches up when she's annoyed. Get her riled up about something silly, so she forgets herself and touches me. I doubted she even noticed she did it. Too busy trying to snatch the book from my hands to notice how she grabbed on to my arm for leverage as she hopped up. The warmth of her hand on my arm was almost as intoxicating as the way she bit her lip in concentration. Each little useless jump pushed more of her dark skin against mine, more of her scent in my nose, until I grew mad enough to pin her against the bookshelf. Gods, the look of desire in her big brown eyes was so beautiful. I almost dropped to my knees and prayed to it. If it wasn't for that damn love potion, would she have let me?

The mere thought of it had me jumping out of the cot to resume my aggravated pacing. There had to be a way to convince her that I was her mate. How humans, or any other creature for that matter, went their whole lives without the rules of a fated mate, was beyond me. How could they pick someone to settle down with if there was no guarantee it would work?

Madness. The divorce rates must be insane. It would have been so much easier if she were a werewolf. One look at me and Brie would know exactly who she belonged to. *She could be, if I bit her.*

"No." I shook my head, banishing the evil thought. Turning someone without their permission was a taboo even I wasn't desperate enough to cross. She could end up hating me for it.

Or she wouldn't. Maybe the call would be just as strong for her. Maybe she'd greet me with open arms and spread her legs for me. Let me worship her cunt and lock her thighs around my head as she screamed. What I wouldn't give to hike up that ridiculous nightgown and bend her over the nearest surface. Just like she said. My little lamb would be loud. I could sense it. She'd moan for my cock and whimper against me as I took her deep.

Blood rushed to my cock as I imagined her bent over the coffee table. I groaned and dragged my hand down its length, giving in to the fantasy. Biting back a growl, I pumped faster, picturing my mate's body pinned underneath me. Her lips parted on a gasp, leaving an opening to taste her, and I'd never deny myself that pleasure. I needed her taste on my tongue more than I needed air in my lungs.

The ship rocked on a wave and my mind turned it into my lamb, flipping us over. Riding me and taking what she wanted. I'd lick my way up her breasts before nibbling on her collarbone. Begging her to use me the way she liked. Demanding she tell me just what to do so I'd have her coming around my cock. I panted and worked myself faster. Dreaming of spilling inside her hot cunt, then lying in the afterglow with her in my arms. We'd spend the rest of the day on a rowboat, gliding aimlessly through the bayou. Chatting about nothing and everything until we stopped on a grassy knoll surrounded by wildflowers, tore our clothes off and fucked again. My heart squeezed painfully in my chest as I chased the image with my own orgasm. *Soon.* I snatched a cloth from the dresser and fisted it around my cock. Spilling my release on the promise of making that dream a reality. It didn't matter if she was human or werewolf. I'd make her see just how right I was for her.

"BARAKU!" The captain's scream brought me back to reality. I sighed and cleaned myself off before heading out to the main hallway of the forecastle.

Our ship's captain, Usha, appeared to be in another one of her fits. Several of my crew members snickered as the enraged woman pounded on the door of another one of the private rooms.

With our co-captain, Cinnamon, gone to live on her farm, Usha was the only human left on the ship. Yet she possessed a fighting demeanor that left her more than capable of herding around a full crew of demons. That, and a vicious right hook. The last fool that tried his luck with her patience nursed a black eye for a week.

Feathers were tangled throughout her dark red mane,

45

courtesy of the terrified chicken she held in one arm. "BARAKU, OPEN THIS DOOR! HOW MANY TIMES DO I HAVE TO TELL YOU TO STOP STEALING ANIMALS?"

Loud shuffling, followed by a "baa" noise, sounded off behind the door. "There are no animals in here!"

"DON'T LIE TO ME, BARAKU!" she screamed again.

"These accusations are false. I stole no goats!"

Usha roared in anger and threw the chicken in my arms. "Hold this," she snapped. Usha backed up from the door before shimming up her long skirts. Then, with a snarl, she kicked the door open.

There, standing hunched over three pygmy goats, was the orc in question. His dark reddish-purple skin was littered with minor scratches and his long, dark hair held even more feathers than Usha's. A small white kitten batted at the ruby dangles of his earrings. Piles of hay littered the floor, along with at least ten different animals. How Baraku managed to smuggle all of them in here without notice was beyond me. Though when it came to his obsession with small creatures, anything was possible.

A goose honked, then ran past the seething captain and darted up the stairs to freedom. Baraku hunched closer around the pygmy goats. "This…this isn't what it looks like!"

Growling low, Usha buried her face in her hands. "I agreed to let you have *one* pet on the ship. Why do I see twelve?"

"They needed a home!"

The captain's hands clenched in front of her in a strangling motion. "Did they need a home, or did you kidnap them from a farm?"

Baraku's mouth opened, but no words came out. He glanced at me, eyes pleading, but I shook my head. Even for him, this was excessive.

"Pick one," Usha demanded.

The orc fidgeted and looked around at his collection. "I can't just pick one."

Her eyes narrowed, and she crossed her arms over her chest. "You can pick one, or I call Kiki and let her pick one too."

Baraku gasped. "You wouldn't!"

Usha brought a hand to the side of her mouth and let out a long whooping noise. Baraku panicked and frantically gathered up creatures in his arms. The telltale sound of paws thudded above deck, making their way to the staircase.

"Wait, we can sort this out!" he pleaded.

The crew and I backed against the walls of the hallway as Kiki, Usha's pet hyena, loped her way down the steps. Upon seeing the menagerie of prey, the beast licked her chops and ran forward. Baraku screeched and held up the small kitten. "Rebekah! I pick Rebekah, call her off!"

Usha held up a hand, and Kiki skittered to a halt at her side. "Return the rest of the animals, or we eat them. Apologize to the farmers while you're at it. They're already having a hard enough time adjusting to our presence without adding thievery on top of it."

Chest heaving, Baraku slumped to the floor, cradling his new kitten. The tiny creature paid no mind to the stress of her master and resumed swatting at his earrings.

"I need a drink," Usha said, leaving Baraku to sort out his mess.

I released the scared chicken and followed her upstairs. "You know it's barely morning, right?"

She waved me off and made a beeline for the barrels of mead stashed in the captain's quarters and filled up a jug. "I'll remember to be properly scandalized when it's not the ass crack of dawn."

Usha poured us both a glass and sank into the plush leather chair behind her desk. With a shrug, I took a seat on the couch and drank. Gods knew I needed it. "So," she began, swirling her glass. "I hear congratulations are in order. You imprinted right?"

I downed the glass without a word.

"Damn, that bad? What did she do, kick you in the nuts?"

"Worse," I muttered. "She spilled a love potion on me and now doesn't believe I've actually imprinted."

Usha poured me another drink. "How do you know if you did? Seems like an awfully big coincidence to imprint the same time you get smacked with a love spell."

"Not you too," I groaned.

She held up her hands in surrender. "I'm just saying, if I was in her shoes I'd be hesitant too."

This is why every species should just imprint and be done with it.

"It's not the love potion. I've been cursed before by Myva's magic and this is different."

"How?"

Dammit all. How do you explain something as bone-deep as an imprint to a creature that doesn't have a comparison to it? "It's like…A curse makes you feel you're far too drunk. You stumble around, not sure of your actions, and your mind feels hazy. You know something isn't right, but there's not much you can do about it. While, yes, I do feel the small haze of the love potion. It's secondary. Minuscule in comparison to the starving sensation I get now that I'm away from her."

Though I didn't want to admit that the love potion was probably making the call to claim my mate much worse. I'd only seen one other werewolf go through the process, but he wasn't this frantic. Each passing second was a gnawing torture at the edge of my consciousness. If I wasn't careful, the next time I saw my lamb, I'd probably scare her off for good.

Usha rested her elbows on her desk, nursing her drink. "Both of those things sound awful, honestly."

"It won't stay this way. I just need to claim her before it gets too bad."

She narrowed her eyes at me. Concern creeping into her stern face. "What happens when it gets too bad?"

I looked away, unsure myself.

"Felix." Her voice dropped low, the tone unmistakably threatening. "If I find out you do something to hurt this woman—"

I held up a hand. "I'd sooner feed myself to a pack of wild dogs." The thought of anyone hurting my mate made my blood boil. Doing it myself was unthinkable. Not that it mattered. She'd come around. I just had to be patient. Calm. Avoid dairy.

Soothed, Usha leaned back in her chair. "Good."

Suddenly, the door burst open, almost coming off its hinges. My brother Balabash ran into the room holding a book. He slammed the door shut and threw himself against the desk. "Usha! Is it true that human women have a sensitive spot just below their cervix that gives intense pleasure?" Before she could even react, Dante and Isaak came barreling in after him.

Dante dipped his head to avoid scraping his horn on the door frame before shoving past Isaak. "Don't forget about the pressure thing." The dragon shifter slammed his hands on the desk, causing Usha to scoot back in her chair. "Does adding pressure to your lower belly increase the sensation of orgasms?"

What?

The poor woman looked so tired. She set her drink down and ran a hand down her face. "Y'all motherfuckers are getting way too comfortable with me."

Dante nodded. "Be that as it may, please confirm if this manual is telling the truth."

She sighed and held out her hand. "Give me the damn book."

Bash handed it over and the trio waited patiently as the captain flipped through its contents. "Where did you even get this?"

Isaak straightened, grinning with pride. "I bought it off a traveling merchant that passed through town two days ago. He promised it held the secrets of pleasing any human woman."

That caught my attention. Before we demons were set free, only a handful of us had hardly ever even seen a woman, let alone gotten the honor of pleasing one. I'd had the occasional dalliance with other men, but the competition for the few demon women around was too much of a bother. I never saw a point in joining the legions of suitors after them if I didn't imprint. But if there was a manual on how to please my mate, I wanted to hear every word.

"Well?" Balabash fidgeted next to her chair, almost knocking into the barrels of mead.

Usha raised an eyebrow and kept reading. "This book knows more about my body than I do."

"So it's true then?" I asked.

Sipping her drink, Usha flipped through another page. "I can confirm the G and A spot dictated in the first few pages, but I haven't even tried half of this stuff." She closed the book and handed it back to the orc. "Seems like you got your money's worth, from what I can tell. Did all of you imprint too?"

Isaak spoke up first. "We orcs don't imprint. But Bal has his eye on a pretty barmaid. I haven't found mine yet, but with so many women in this realm, I want to be ready!"

"And you?" she asked Dante.

The dragon glowered. "No. But like he said, the possibility is no longer a fool's errand. Now that things are mostly settled, I'll set off to find my mate soon. It feels odd staying in another dragon's territory, anyway."

The Storm Dragon must have been burning with jealousy for Fallon. The Shadow Dragon was hundreds of years younger than him, but had already found his mate and claimed Boohail and the surrounding bayou as his new territory. It only made sense. Cinnamon's family was all here. Dante would most likely just lay claim to whatever village he found his own woman in. Dragons were simple like that.

Though it was strange to see two in the same place for so long. Or see one at all. Before escaping Volsog, Bash and the rest of our clan lived under the Stone Dragon's territory in the East Coast region. But in the twenty-seven years we'd been there, I couldn't recall seeing him once. As far as overlords went, he was completely hands-off. The only rule being to never step foot in the large cave system he called home.

Perhaps now that we were no longer held captive by the limited resources of that frozen wasteland, Fallon didn't feel the need to reinforce strict borders. The thought was a strange but pleasant one. Dragon borders were so absolute that maps had to be redrawn anytime one died or was defeated by another. The fact that I was now on a first-name basis with not one but two of the titan creatures was proof of the dawn of a new era. One where women didn't die from Myva's curse.

"Let me see that book." Not bothering to hide my excitement, I snatched it from Bash and began reading.

"Careful, don't scratch it!" Isaak's vast form loomed over me, as if I were about to shred the book into tatters.

"I'm not going to scratch it. Calm down."

Dante came up to my side and peered over my shoulder. "Flip to the page about erogenous zones. I have questions."

"I need more female friends," Usha groaned, downing her glass.

I shifted from one foot to another and eyed the dragon. "Dante, I heard Fallon placed a rune on himself that keeps him from getting Cin pregnant. Do you know how to do that, too?"

The silver-haired man furrowed his brow. "A barren rune? Yes, they're easy to conjure. Most dragons keep them on until we want to have children."

"Is it possible for you to give me one? My Brie looked taken aback when I asked how many kids she wanted."

Usha choked on her mead and shook her head.

"Yes," Dante said, rolling up his sleeves. "We can do it now if you're ready." Sparks ignited from his wrists and danced up the dragon shifter's arms.

That looks concerning. "How long does it take?"

He averted his gaze and tilted his head. "Just lift up your shirt and it will be over quickly."

The uncharacteristically light tone in his voice planted a seed of worry in my gut. "How quickly?"

"Just a quick zap and you're done." He advanced a step forward. I took one back.

"Does it hurt?" The hair on the back of my neck stood up as I noticed the corner of his mouth twitch as if he was fighting off a grin.

"A little. No more than a sting. Just don't look at it."

"Are you lying to me?"

Dante paused. The air became thick with tension. Balabash, Isaak, and Usha watched on in silence. "No."

"Alright," I said. Dante's gray eyes took on a sadistic glint and the grin he'd been hiding came out in full force. It was then I knew that I fucked up.

Without giving me time to react, the dragon shifter lifted my shirt and jabbed me in the lower gut, just above my right hip. I yelped at the initial shock, but the sharp sting soon faded. I blinked and held a hand to the rune.

"Well, that wasn't so bad," I said.

Burning pain shot from my torso down to my toes. I fell forward onto my knees, screaming.

"It might be more than a sting," Dante muttered.

"OH YOU LIED. YOU LYING SACK OF CLOUD SCALES!"

Dante threw back his head and laughed as I rolled on the

floor. "Chin up, wolf, it's a rite of passage amongst young drag-ons. You should be honored."

"THIS HONOR IS RIPPING THROUGH MY SKIN LIKE THE POISON OF A BASILISK. YOU SICK WARLOCK OF PAIN!"

"I know," he chuckled. "It's heinous. I've never gotten to do it to anyone else before." He turned to Isaak and Balabash. "Who's next?"

The two orcs edged toward the door in fear. Dante crouched forward, as if to pounce. "Oh, don't be cowards." His tone was mocking, the same threatening grin present. "It's a lot less painful than what your woman would go through if you put her through childbirth. You can't expect her to go through worse pain if you yourself can't even offer her this."

"That's a fair point," I heard Usha say. "Get 'em, Dante!"

With a grunt, I wrapped my arms around his legs and held tight. "Don't listen to him. Run!"

He tried to lunge at the fleeing men, but fell just short of snatching Isaak by his braids.

Dante sighed as the two frantically ran out the door. "You're no fun," he said, turning to me.

"You're evil," I growled.

He held out a hand to help me up, and I took it. The pain finally ebbing away. "Maybe. But I'm sure your mate will thank me for it."

His words mollified my anger a little. If Brie wasn't ready to start a family, then the stress of pregnancy was probably a heavy weight over her head. While that was undoubtedly one of the worst pains I'd ever felt, it was over rather quickly. I'm still going to get him back one day, though.

"Captain," a voice called from outside. "There's a group of angry men trying to board the ship. They want to speak with you."

"It's just one thing after another," Ursa muttered and made her way to the deck. I followed close behind, looking for any and all distractions to keep me from running back to Brie's home and begging her to let me try out the book's suggestions and my new rune. If I was ever going to gain her trust, I at least needed to give her space. As terrible of a concept it was.

Balabash went forward first and waited near the ship's entry. His intimidating size was enough to keep the gaggle of angry men planted firmly on the dock. They scowled and clenched their pitchforks and axes, but none dared to step on the bridge to challenge him.

"They seem like a friendly bunch," I said.

Usha sighed beside me and placed a hand on my shoulder. I didn't have to turn around to feel the burning glare Ambrose sent my way. The lamia was never far from the captain. Watching over to make sure some unfortunate man didn't make the mistake of staring at her too long. "Felix, you and Holly are the only other two sane people on this ship. And she's off fucking that hero girl somewhere. Please don't let me lose my temper on these men."

Feeling mischievous, I threw an arm around her shoulders and smiled in Ambrose's direction. "So long as you keep your bodyguard from tearing off my limbs."

Ambrose was a stoic man and hardly ever showed any emotion on his face. Someone who didn't know him well would probably think he'd just been staring off into space. But if you were paying attention, you would notice the way his fingers dug into his palms or the way his snake half coiled just a little tighter into himself, like a viper ready to strike. The brief hints of anger were barely there, but that just made him all the more fun to tease. And I did it often.

She threw a look back at him and rolled her eyes. "He'll be fine." Taking a deep breath, Usha shook me off and donned a friendly smile. "Gentlemen, to what do we owe the pleasure?"

A balding man with an ax stepped forward. "Two of our women went missing last night! We know it was your damn demons who took them! We will not stand by as you heathens take our women in the night to boil in your soups. Hand them over now!"

A chorus of shouts sounded off behind him. Each of the men shook their pitiful weapons in the air. I doubted it would be much effort for even one of us to take out the lot of them. But we were trying to build a community here. And it wouldn't do to go off killing villagers every time one shook a pitchfork at us.

"That's ridiculous!" Lothur shouted. The minotaur stomped

his way to the side of the ship and snorted. "Females are rare and precious. None of us would ever hurt one!"

"But you would take them!" the man shouted. "That's why you're here, isn't it? There's only one female demon in your crew, so you monsters have set out to take ours!"

"Who went missing?" Balabash asked. His face turned ashen as he scanned the docks. "Who is gone? Is it my Sunbeam?"

Cold fear shot down my spine at his words. Could Brie have been taken after I left? I spent so much time trying to keep away from her that I left her completely undefended. The surrounding voices continued to shout at each other, but they grew farther and farther away as darkness clouded my thoughts.

I left her. I left her and she could be in danger. She could be dead.

Usha took my hand in hers and squeezed. Grounding me back to reality. She held her head high and addressed the leader of the group. "My men would never steal anyone. But you are free to search the ship with me. What are their names?"

The balding man grinned, as if he'd won some sort of prize. "Serena and Kitty."

Not Brie or Sunbeam. Thank the stars.

I turned to Bash, who nodded. As soon as the human men left the ship, we'd check on them both. It was fortunate that Bash had found his mate at the same time as I did. Orcs didn't imprint like werewolves, but they had a certain knowing about them and were fiercely protective.

Some males even choose to pursue a woman as a group for better protection.

Even if we were separate species, Bash and I were raised together after his father took me in. There was no one in the world I could count on more. We'd help look for the missing women and destroy whoever thought to harm them in the first place.

Brie and Sunbeam are fine. I'm fine.

I'm fine.

But when the men searched the ship and came up empty-handed, we helped them search the docks—only to find nothing. We searched Serena's and Kitty's homes and found no trace. Not even my superior nose could trace them anywhere in the village. With each dead end, my nerves became more fried. Worse still, a frantic mother had approached the search party to inform us that her daughter had gone missing as well. All women were in their twenties. All unmarried. Gone without a trace.

I'm not fine.

A frantic Balabash crashed through the door of Sunbeam's home above her bar. She was livid, but safe. The orc crushed her to him, breathing a sigh of relief as she swatted at his face. "What is wrong with you?" she snapped.

"Sunbeam, my beautiful sunflower. I thought you were taken in the night!" The red orc looked near tears as he checked the barmaid for any signs of injury.

After explaining the morning's events, the woman calmed and allowed Bash to search her home for any signs of trouble. What should have been relief only turned to more fear in my gut. Sunbeam was safe. But was Brie?

Chapter 4

Brie

Marriage was a strange beast. Or maybe it was just Cinnamon's marriage. "Beloved," my friend said, her shoulders slumping in exasperation. "You don't grow facial hair. What am I supposed to shave?"

Fallon glared at his wife from his spot in the doorway. Their home had been updated with larger frames to accommodate his freakishly tall stature. But he still looked like a giant in the quaint little cottage. The smoke rising from his arms made me concerned for the ancient-looking books in his hands. He was sent to retrieve any books Cin's ma had on magic. But if he didn't calm down, that task would burn to cinders. "We could still go through the motions of it. Your father said it was an important bonding ritual between him and your mother."

She put an elbow on the kitchen table and rested her chin in her hand. "Pa can grow a beard."

More smoke rose from the dragon shifter. "Maybe you could trim his hair?" I offered, desperate to find common ground before it was too late.

Cin shook her head. "You don't cut a dragon's hair. It's a sign of defeat."

Dammit woman, work with me. "Fallon, put the books down if you're about to burst into flames again."

He growled low in his throat, but did as instructed. Slamming the three large tomes on the table. I let out a sigh of relief when I saw that the leather-bound covers looked undamaged. The top of the stack had bright blue letters spelling out "Magic, Hexes, And You." Fallon took a seat next to his wife, took the top book, and began flipping through it, not looking at her.

Calmly, Cin sipped her coffee and eyed her husband. "Don't pout."

His tone was flat as he flipped past another page. "I am not pouting."

"Of course," she said. "You know, it's not just shaving. We consider any form of hair care a bonding ritual around here. Right Brie?"

"Yep," I said, grabbing the next book. Whatever put an end to his weird mood. "The Nitwit's Guide To Fortune-Telling" looked well used. Its pale leather bindings were loose on the seams, and a few paper bookmarks poked out the top. Mrs. Hotpepper must have spent weeks going through every page. The woman collected stories and tales from every corner of the world she could, and when she couldn't find any more through the merchants that traveled through Boohail, she turned to fortune telling. Desperate to snatch even more tales from the future. Her favorite myths and legends could be found tattooed on her person. In case she ever forgot them. When she ran out of room, Cin's father happily offered up his back to store more stories.

"Do you want me to braid your hair later?" Cin asked.

Fallon's shoulders relaxed. The crease in his brow faded away with his answer. "Yes."

Cin smiled and patted his arm before grabbing the remaining book, "Hexing For Fun And Profit."

"Did Ma have anything to say about removing love potions?"

Fallon turned his book around to show us the page he'd stopped on. "She mentioned Kinnamo's creation story might have reference to a similar situation. Legend says a werebear had fallen victim to a powerful love potion and chased after the wife of a water dragon."

Hope bloomed in my chest. If this wasn't the first instance of a love spell gone wrong, then maybe there was a quicker way to put an end to it. "Did they find a way to reverse the spell?" I asked.

"No." He shrugged. "The werebear ends up going mad and killing her. Then the water dragon floods the continent in a fit of rage. Creating the bayou that exists today."

Cinnamon glared. "Love. That is not helping."

He turned the book back to him and scanned the pages. "I never said it was a nice creation story. There's a reason love potions and any magic specializing in mind-altering effects is strictly banned for our kind. Humans have a natural resistance to magic, so the risks aren't as great for you. But Brie should know what she's gotten into. The effects of the love potion are only going to get worse as the days go on. If he's truly imprinted on top of that, then we'd have no way of telling how bad it's going to get. The man could just drop dead of a heart attack because of the strain."

My stomach twisted into knots. "I thought it was bad enough when he broke into my house."

Cin and Fallon paused from their reading. "He what?" Cin asked.

Fallon's tone took on a frosted edge. One that made me sit up a little straighter in fear. "Are you alright, did he hurt you in any way?"

"No," I blurted. "Well, it started with him breaking in to bring me home after I fainted on the road home. Then, instead of leaving, he did a bunch of chores and just kinda stayed over. We had breakfast, but I think he had an allergic reaction to the grilled cheese and ran off. But aside from that, nothing bad." I left out the part where I was backed up against my bookshelf by the sexiest man I'd ever seen, as he lamented about not being able to shove his tongue down my cunt. A girl had to have her privacy, after all. I fiddled with the ends of my long twists, trying to wrest away the imagery.

"You fainted? Are you alright now?" Cin asked.

I nodded. "Some weird gator thing attacked me, but Felix took care of it." Cin let out a breath of relief, then shared a look with her husband. The couple burst out into laughter. Fallon tucked away the long black hair that fell in front of his face before clenching at his side. "I'm never going to let him live that down."

"I can't believe he willingly ate cheese!" Cin giggled around her mug.

"Snapping gators, the man must have been privy-bound the rest of the day."

Irritation replaced the worried knots in my gut. Was I really so intimidating that he couldn't ask for something else? "If he knew he was allergic to cheese, then why did he eat it?"

Fallon regained his composure enough to answer. "You could have set a plate of broken glass in front of him and he would have eaten it to please you. He won't be able to help himself. Until the curse is broken, you'll need to be careful about what you say to him."

"You two seem awfully calm about this. Shouldn't you be concerned if your friend could drop dead of a heart attack, or you know, KILL ME?" I asked.

Cinnamon shrugged. "I just get the feeling it's going to work out. Felix is so easygoing and seems like the perfect match for you. Besides, you've always gravitated toward those werewolf romance novels. If this isn't fate smacking you in the face, then I don't know what is."

"Reading choices aside," Fallon cut in, "we've caught this in the early stages. If these books don't have the answer for a removal spell, then you can always just yield to the love potion's demands until the effect wears off."

"What do you mean?" I asked.

"You sleep with him," the dragon said, as if it were the most obvious thing in the land. "It may even wear off after that. I've seen a few spells that were condition-based. That sniveling whelp who bought it wasn't much help information-wise, so I'm not sure what the full effects are. All he could tell us is that he bought it from a merchant in Doncaster."

"I can't just fuck him on the off chance it will work. He's under a spell, so that's dubious consent, at best." The thought of it only made me even angrier at Jack. That piece of shit knew exactly what he was doing, and now Felix was paying the price for it.

My friend patted my shoulder, trying to soothe my apprehension. "You're right Brie, but if it were me, and my options were heart attack or sex, I'd choose sex."

"Try not to dwell on that for now," Fallon said, relaxing into his chair. "This book has an entire chapter dedicated to spell removal. When you get him alone, you can try each of them out. If they don't work, then come back here and we can plan the next step. I know little about hormonal magic, but our friend Dante might. He's much older than I am and may have more insight."

"Alone?" Goosebumps raced down my arms. "You're not coming with me? I don't know a thing about magic."

Fallon nodded in sympathy. "I know. But this type of magic causes deep emotional strain on the victim. When the extraction starts, Felix will grow desperate and will most likely view anyone else in the room as a threat to his mate. If he lashes out at either of us, it will put more strain on his heart and could lead to his death."

I buried my head in my hands. "Well, damn." *This is just fucking great.*

The trek back to my farm gave me a chance to sort out my thoughts. Felix and I were strangers, but I wasn't about to let the man keel over because I threw a drink at his head. It wouldn't be my first one-night stand either. Boohail was a great place to live and grow up, but it was slim pickings as far as men went. The occasional trip to neighboring towns for different dick was one of the few ways you didn't get desperate enough to saddle yourself to the closest boring man without a wife. Or worse. One of those idiot Huckabee boys. Every day would be a never-ending nightmare of fish, misogyny and bad manners. Several women in Boohail, myself included, had decided we'd rather die alone long ago.

I shivered, banishing the thought from my head by focusing instead on the smell of fresh rain. With fall in full swing, small showers often broke out throughout the day. Not that I minded. There was something calming about the sound of wet leaves under your boot. Calming was something I was going to need a lot of.

Squeezing the magic book closer to my chest, I tilted my head back and allowed the scent to wash over me. Pumpkins lined the fields at the edge of Cin's property, almost bleeding into mine. Round and fat with seeds just waiting to be cooked and eaten. Old oak trees curved along the sides of the road, forming a tunnel of wonders set ablaze by red and orange leaves. It stretched on for miles, blocking just enough sun with its foliage to form dancing stars on the cobblestones below. As children, Cin, Cherry, and I would run through them as fast as we could. Thinking a portal would open up to take us to some magical place. If I could go back and tell them that I was currently holding a magic book, on my way to save a werewolf, they may have passed out from excitement.

What I wouldn't give to be that carefree again. Where everything was new and exciting, and the three of us together and safe. Maybe it wasn't too late. Cherry was gone, but the rest of us were still here. And Cin's husband was a fucking dragon. Not only that, but a ship full of magical creatures was currently docked at our port. Most of them were looking to make a home for themselves on our shores.

Taking a deep breath, I reminded myself that magic was not only real, but right in front of me. I could do this. I could save Felix one way or another.

If the curse lifts and he still thinks I'm his fated mate, then great.

*Free husband. In time, I think he'll be someone easy to love. If not...
well that might sting a little. But maybe he'll introduce me to his friends.*

Just be calm.

Be cool.

Don't stare too deeply into the ocean of his eyes.

Confidence renewed, I made my way home to wait for him.
If what he said was true, then Felix's need to be near me
would drag him back to my doorstep soon enough. Yellow
roses sprawled against the surrounding oak trees near my
farm's entrance. Their mad dash to the sun left no room for
competitors in their wake. Nearly covering the Shields name
plate I'd proudly hung up once I'd bought the land in full from
Mr. Hotpepper.

Hold on.

There were no roses covering my name plate. My name was
gone. In its place sat a freshly carved sign nestled in between
roses trimmed in an orderly fashion. "Who the fuck is Monet?"

"We are, sweetheart."

I whirled around to see Felix looking a little worse for wear.
His clothes were crumpled up and smothered with dirt. Dark
circles made his eyes look sunken, and yet the same cheery grin
still lit up his face. He reached a hand out before tucking it back
into his pocket. "Felix...hi," I said, ever the master of words.

His grin rose to a full smile. He shifted his weight back and
forth before I saw his fist twitch in his pocket. The imagery of
an excited dog doing its best not to jump on its master came

to mind. I guess I should be grateful he's not in werewolf form this time.

"So listen, don't be mad," he began. But the words cut off. He grit his teeth and ran a hand through his hair. The wavy blond locks almost snagging against his fingers. Nostrils flaring, he growled. "Forgive me."

Before I could even flinch, Felix crushed me to his chest. Strong arms held me to him like a vice, as if I'd melt away if he didn't hold on tight enough. I shivered as he buried his nose in my hair, inhaling deeply. I tried to lean back and pull away, but stopped when I felt him shaking. "Are you alright?" I asked.

"Not in the slightest," he whispered against my temple. "Just let me stay here for a bit. I'll pull myself together in a moment."

Relaxing in his hold, I shifted the book to my side so it would stop jabbing me in the gut. "Did something happen?" Was the magic getting worse? The man looked like he hadn't slept in a week.

He didn't answer for a moment, and I waited patiently for his body to stop shaking. "Three women went missing. We've been searching for them all day, but there's no trace. When I didn't find you home, I thought you might be gone too."

"What?" Cold fear splashed through me. This was such a small village, how could no one notice three women just vanishing?

He squeezed tighter until I felt the rapid beat of his heart against my cheek. "I shouldn't have left you."

"Felix, I'm fine. Well, I can't breathe, but I'm fine." His death grip finally loosened at my words, but he kept a hand on the small of my back. Despite my fear of the distressing news, a small selfish part of me felt happy. No one had ever worried about me like this. Deriving pleasure from his disheveled appearance was undoubtedly sick and probably said terrible things about my character. Nevertheless, a small bloom of butterflies tickled in my tummy.

Stomp them down, Brie. You little pervert.

"Do you have any idea why they could have been taken?" I asked.

He shook his head. "All we could find out was that they were all unmarried and in their twenties. The men in the village think it could have been a roaming band of demons, but I would have scented them around the area."

Unmarried women in their twenties. The butterflies turned to stones as I glanced back at the sign. The sign that was no longer my name.

Felix scratched the back of his head and looked down sheepishly. "This is where I need you to try not to get mad."

"What did you do?"

"I may have...gone down to the courthouse and registered us as a married couple."

I blinked. "How? You shouldn't be able to do that without me. Don't we both need to sign and say vows to a priest or something?"

"Well yes. That's what the clerk said at first."

"At first?" I asked, not liking where this was going.

"At first," he nodded. "But with the church being burned down, and you know…the economy."

"Felix," I said, impatience bleeding into my voice.

"Well, it turns out if you show up with claws, fangs, and three orcs, they'll let you do just about anything." His tone lightened, like someone who found a great bargain on fleece at the market.

Dizziness made me sway on my feet. "We're married?"

"Yes," he said, almost hesitant.

"Like…married, married?"

Felix tilted his head. "Do humans have multiple kinds of marriages?"

I'm married. To a man I met no less than three days ago. A man who holds up the courthouse with a gaggle of merry fucking orcs. "I need a drink."

"I think that would be wise, yes." He guided me down the walkway of my (our?) home. My mind was reeling, just focusing on putting one foot in front of the other. "Lamb?"

"Yes?" I asked.

"I know I've pushed well past all sense of boundaries, but I have one request."

"Shoot."

His gaze drifted to mine, a light pink blush across his face. "Can I carry you over the threshold?"

Sighing, I stopped in front of the door. "Fuck it, why not?"

Chapter 5

Felix

The gods must have been testing me. If so, I was losing terribly. Why else would my mate willingly let a crazed man into her home?

Alone.

After yielding to my selfish desire to carry her across the threshold to celebrate the marriage forced upon her. Then, as if by some cruel joke, provided me with a robe to wear after drawing a bath. A robe she handmade. It smelled like fucking jasmine.

And we're alone.

I shifted in my seat in her living room, checking to make sure she hadn't returned before sneaking another whiff at the garment. *She's not getting this back. It's mine now.*

"Sorry for the wait," she called from the kitchen. I sat up straighter and dropped the sleeve. Not that it mattered. Any attempt to not look like a deranged lunatic went out the window when she stepped into the room.

Brie had changed into a robe of her own. One where the only thing holding it together was the flimsiest-looking string I'd ever seen. The evening sun filtered through the peaks of lavender curtains to dance on the graceful slope of her neck. My throat went dry as my gaze followed its neckline, dipped low, exposing the tops of her plump breasts. I snatched a pillow from the side of the love seat and covered my rising cock. I wasn't sure how much my own robe would cover, but judging by the flare in her wide hips, it wasn't enough.

Brie set a pair of wine glasses down on the table and sat across from me. Her warm floral scent filled the room until I could just about taste her in the air. I closed my eyes for a moment, beating away the thought of reaching over the table and snatching the robe off her. It would be safer if I stayed outside. She'd still be safe from intruders if I slept in the barn and patrolled the property. Being this close sent my blood on fire, and my little lamb clearly had no idea of the damage she was doing to my psyche.

I'm calm. I'm fine.

"I do not know how this is going to go. So I think I should just be honest." She grabbed a large book off the table and patted the cover. "According to Fallon, we need to get this love spell off you as soon as possible, or you might die." She bit her lip and glanced away. A worried crease worked its way into her brow. "And if none of these removal spells work…then we're going to have to have sex."

Phaaos, God of Love, Lust, and Hunt, I will place a kill at your altar every week until my dying breath. I cleared my throat. The table was only two and a half feet at best. It would be nothing to reach her across from it. "That…seems like a brilliant plan. I have no complaints." *We can just skip to the end. Why wait, honestly? Waiting is stupid. That string is. So. Snappable.*

Brie snorted and put a hand to her mouth before giggling. "That's kind of the problem," she said. "I want to avoid that if possible. We still don't know if it's you who wants that or the love potion."

I leaned back in my chair, trying to smooth the desperate eagerness in my voice. "Ah yes, my precious virtue. I assure you, Lamb, I'm completely fine."

She raised an eyebrow. "Remove the pillow."

Damn. "Well played."

"Look, we at least have to try. If it doesn't work, then we can do it your way." Brie flipped to a bookmarked page and ran a finger down the text.

Anger burned through me, and I looked away. *This is ridiculous. I am not jealous of paper.* But I wanted her hands on me. I wanted to skip her silly book of spells, throw her down on her bed and finally ease this all-consuming ache threatening to eat me alive. *Alright. Maybe it's partially the love potion taking over. But still. Fuck that page.*

Brie sipped her drink as she continued to scan over the book. "Do you want to start now, or wait until tomorrow? You look like you could use a good night's rest."

She uncrossed her legs, then re-crossed them, changing her right to be on top. It was only a moment, a second. But the barest peak of her inner thigh teased its way into my growing insanity. What I wouldn't give to run my tongue along the rich length of her dark skin. Trail my way up her body and—

"Felix?"

I shook my head. "I'm sorry, love. What did you say?"

She held my gaze, no doubt wondering if I'd keel over that very second. "Do you want to sleep first? If the love potion isn't too bad, we can do this tomorrow."

"Can I sleep with you?" I am nothing if not an opportunist.

Amusement lit in her eyes, but she kept her face impassive. If I wasn't so enthralled with every move she made, Brie would have made an excellent gambler. But I was. So the subtle shift in her eyes didn't escape my notice. Nor did the tip of her wine glass as she loosened her grip. She was thinking about it.

Say yes. Please. I could be good for a night. What's an aching cock compared to getting closer to my mate? Nothing. I knew she wanted to keep me at an emotional distance. It was smart, considering the drug. But dammit, I wasn't going to let her. Brie was mine. Her caution was mine to ease. Her bed was mine to fill and—fuck everything—I just wanted to fucking touch her.

"I don't think that's wise," she sighed.

I grinned at her and raised my hands in surrender. "I promise not to ravish you in the night. We can put a wall of pillows up, if that would help."

She widened her eyes and nodded. "Oh, of course, a wall of pillows. The one true way to stop a werewolf! Why didn't I think of that?"

Leaning forward, I clapped my hands together as if revealing a dastardly plan. "We're a team now, beloved. We come to solutions together."

"You're impossible," she said, laughing.

"No, I'm just in love with you," I said.

Her laughter stopped, and she set down her glass. "Right, spell removal it is, then."

"Is it really so unbelievable?"

"A little," she began. "And while yes, a fated-mate-type situation would do wonders for my abandonment issues, I'm just not that lucky."

Rage festered deep in my bones. If my Lamb's reserved demeanor resulted from a past lover, then whatever fool it was would need to be dealt with. "Who abandoned you, sweetheart? I'll bring you his head."

"Whoa there, killer. I appreciate the offer, but I doubt having my dad's head on a pike will be that great of a closure." She tucked a loose black curl behind her ear. Her gaze drifted to the floorboards as if looking at some far-off memory.

"We won't know unless we try," I said, playfully.

The reward was instant. Her nose crunched up before she attempted to cover another snort with her hand. I closed my eyes, savoring the sound of her laughter. Every day could be like this. Just chatting and laughing and finding out more about each other. "Do you want to tell me about him?" I asked.

She waved me off, trying to reel in the remaining giggles. "There's not much to tell. My family has never been close. One day, my dad left to deliver goods to a neighboring town and didn't come back. In retrospect, we should have probably been tipped off by the extra clothes and supplies." She shrugged her shoulders. "But what can ya do? I was only five or six, so I don't even remember him much."

Desperate to keep her smiling, words flooded out of my mouth like vomit. "Maybe he didn't abandon you. It's possible he was just eaten by an alligator or something." *Stupid. Why would you say that? That's terrible.*

She paused. "You know, that kinda makes me feel better." *Oh. OK, never mind. That worked.*

"Is your family close?" Brie asked. "You mentioned you wanted ten kids, which I'm sorry, but no," she said, fanning herself. "Ten is too many, even if we are fated mates."

I sipped my wine, eager to find out the acceptable number. "Yes, the orc clan I grew up with was all very close. Most of us were scattered during the last run of Myva's curse. But you've met my brother, Balabash. I'm sure our brother Yala will turn up soon. He's always had a knack for hunting us down if we ever got separated."

"Hmm. Yes, I remember Balabash. He's rather taken with Sunbeam. Do werewolves and orcs normally live together?"

"No, I'm adopted. I do not know what happened to my birth parents. But it doesn't matter. The Monet clan is my family. How many kids do you want?"

Brie clutched her drink to her chest. "You're not going to let that question slide, are you?" When I shook my head, she continued. "Maybe three?"

The fact that I'd gone from the possibility of zero to three was promising. "I can work with that."

"You better," she said, narrowing her eyes. "You won't be the one pushing them out." A startled look crossed her face, and she slammed her glass on the table. "Wait, how did we get into this conversation? We're supposed to be removing your curse!" she said, wagging her finger at me. "Stop distracting me."

"I promise nothing." Our future children depended on it.

"Brat," she muttered, returning her attention to the enormous book.

The spell book looked ancient and a little ominous. Most of my kind knew firsthand how dangerous magic could be. Volsog was a frozen hell-scape most of the year. The last thing anyone wanted was to make things worse with magic gone awry. Unless you were born with a natural instinct for it, like fox-shifters or fae, it wasn't something you dared mess with.

"Beloved, not that I don't trust you with my life, but do you know what you're doing?"

"Not at all," she said. "But Fallon said it was a do-or-die situation, so let's give it a try."

"Wasn't fucking our way out of this also an option?" Panic crept up my spine. There was no telling the damage one could do with untested magic. Flashes of waking up, confused and beaten, entered my mind. I didn't even know how much time I lost under Myva's curse. My time spent captured in Wandermere was all a blank until Cinnamon woke me up. It could have been days or weeks.

Brie stood, waving me off. "Fucking our way out is Plan B. OK, first up is the herb blend. Hold still."

She reached into her pocket and pulled out a small leather bag. Shifting the book to rest on her hip, Brie pulled open the bag's drawstring with her teeth and threw it at me. It landed square on my chest, dumping a mix of ground-up spices all over my lap. I looked at the mess, then to her.

She bit her lip and waited. "Well, how do you feel?"

"...dirty?"

"No, no, about me!" she said, patting her chest.

"Oh, I think we should spend the day in a rowboat surrounded by lilies and cuddling." I glanced outside. "There's still a few hours of daylight left. We could pack a few sandwiches and have a picnic. Though if you don't mind, I'll make mine cheese-free."

My lamb buried her head in her hand. "Alright, so nothing. Great."

I brushed off the spice and grinned up at her. "I mean, if it means that much to you, I'll eat another grilled cheese."

Growling, Brie flipped to another page. "No more stomach Armageddon!" she hissed. "Next time, just tell me when you don't like something. I felt terrible for feeding you something that made you sick."

She was worried about me?

"This next page says I have to sing a chant. Don't laugh," she warned.

I raised my glass. "Serenade me, my sweet." Her nose scrunched, making my heart swell. She hunched into the book, clearly trying to hide the embarrassed look on her face. Magic folly and consequences aside, there was nothing that could have pulled me away from letting her perform any manner of magic mishaps. So long as she remained adorable.

I bit the inside of my cheek. Refusing the laugh at the caterwauling that came next. If there were any birds in the area, they'd surely fled out of fear at the sound. A beautiful singer my lamb was not. Sipping my drink, I relaxed on the love seat, clapping when she finally finished. "Beautiful, my darling."

She stomped her foot and snarled. "Oh, don't you patronize me! Are you out of love yet?"

"We should add rocking chairs to the front porch so we can watch the sunset together every evening. How do you feel about the name Rowan? That's our first son. Hopefully, he'll inherit your strong stomach. Most werewolves I know have issues with dairy. I imagine hybrid children will have a stronger disposition. Cheese pups, if you will."

This is too fun.

She paced back and forth, muttering angrily to herself. "Stupid magic books and their shitty spells."

"Just so you're aware, I've received a barren rune from the Storm Dragon, Dante. So we don't have to worry about pregnancy yet. You know, for when we get to Plan B."

If my love were a dragon, she'd be smoking. "Don't count your chickens just yet! I'm not done."

"Of course not, dearest. You're doing great," I said, giving her a thumbs up. She peered over her pages to glare at me. "I hate you so much right now."

I leaned forward, resting my elbows on my knees, and winked at her. "You're so cute when you're mad."

Sputtering, Brie raised the book high. "Oh, I could just throw this book at your head!"

A small chuckle escaped me. "Is that your love language? You seem to love throwing things at me."

She batted her hand in my direction. "I'm ignoring you. Just stay in that chair and don't move. This next one looks like a doozy."

"But darling, my heart!" I teased, clutching at my chest. "I'll die without your love and affection."

"You're gonna love my foot in your ass," she whispered under her breath.

"What was that, Lamb?"

"Ignoring you!" She stomped to the center of her living room and planted her feet firmly. I watched as she bent her knees and began chanting again. This time, accompanying the singing with a little dance. Brie twirled and jumped, chanting her little heart out for a good few minutes. She was left bent over and panting when the spell was finally complete. A hopeful expression crossed her face as she looked back at me.

Just as I was about to spout off another confession of love, a tingle worked its way down my spine. It spread warmth throughout my body and gave me a strange sense of power. "Hold on," I said, setting my glass down. "I think I feel something."

"Really?" Her face brightened. She took a step toward me, only to be knocked off balance as the house rumbled. Paintings and woven ornaments fell from the walls as the ground shook. The scent of fear radiated from Brie as she stumbled amongst the chaos.

I jumped and ran to her, but when I reached my hand out, massive black tentacles erupted from the shadows of the room. Brie screamed as they wove around her and snatched her up. Her fluffy lavender robe fell open as a tentacle wrapped around her belly, while another grabbed her by the leg. They lurched her up, just out of reach, and stopped completely. "What the hell is this?" she cried.

Reaching out again, I noticed the tentacles followed the movement, bringing her closer to me. The strange feeling of power grew stronger.

Brie's mouth fell open before her brows furrowed. "Son of a swan's mistress, you can control them?"

As if in response, another tentacle trailed its way up the rich expanse of her thigh. My breath hitched as it squeezed around it, sinking into the soft cushions of her umber skin.

More.

I needed to see more. With the tie to her robe fallen away, my lamb's body was on full display. From the lush expanse of her legs, to the valley of her breasts, to the tender nape of her neck. I swallowed and watched as a smaller tendril curved around her left breast before it gave a gentle flick against her nipple. The dark bud hardened and peeked under the soft ministrations.

Brie's frustrated snarl shook me out of my thoughts. "Great!" she yelled. "This is just great. Of course, I'd fuck this up bad enough to summon a tentacle monster." She snarled again and thrashed about, then sighed and went limp against the restraints.

I ran a hand over my eyes, trying to calm down. The beat of my heart was pounding in my ears. Yet all blood was directed firmly south. *Get away from her. I need to get the hell away from her before I do something stupid.* Ignoring every base instinct I had, I turned and took a step away from Brie.

My chest lurched, sending me to my knees. The pounding

grew louder until all I could hear was the ferocious thump in my chest. It ripped at my insides like a thousand tiny needles. I dug my claws into the rug, desperate to fight off the urge to transform. My fangs elongated, and I snapped my mouth shut before she could see. The wolf form itched under my skin, ready to break free. All the while, my heart hammered away in my chest. Drowning all thoughts in the cacophony of beating drums.

Over the chaos, Brie's scent called out to me like a beacon. Easing the madness with gentle encouragement to come closer. I did. Helpless to resist the siren's call. My lamb looked so beautiful, even in her anger. A swarm of magic tentacles held the woman hostage, and yet she still managed an impassive glare. As if it was my fault that the spell failed. Maybe it was. Maybe my all-consuming lust for her willed this dream into life. I crawled closer, needing to bury my face in that scent. Surely a taste wouldn't hurt. Just something small, to ease the ache.

"Is my beauty sending you into cardiac arrest?" Brie asked sarcastically.

It took a moment to remember how to form words. "Something like that." I sat back on my haunches and the tendrils holding her up moved her closer. Until her exposed form was mere inches from my face. Swallowing, I let my eyes roam over the warmth of her skin. Down the silken valley of breasts, the soft curves of her stomach, until I greedily settled on her cunt. She squirmed a little under my gaze until the scent of her arousal hit me like a slap. The frantic beat of my heart picked up once more. Without thinking, I reached for her. "Brie," I sighed, my hands just hovering over her hips. She was so close. *Get up. Get up and get out.*

She let out a breath and slumped against the restraints. "Alright. Plan B it is then."

I looked up, but she refused to meet my eye.

I must have heard wrong. "What did you say?"

Her lips pouted, and she kept her gaze anywhere but on me. "I can hear your heart beating like crazy. We tried the stupid book of spells, and it didn't work. So we may as well go with Plan B."

Instinct and reason raged a brutal war. Reason, being a cunning bitch, pulled the win out of thin air. "But you don't want this. Lamb, I can hang on longer. I'm not touching you unless you want it." It was hard. It was awful. But I dropped my hands away from her hips and fisted them at my sides.

She rolled her eyes. "Look, I said no because I'm trying to do the right thing and not take advantage of you while you're under a love spell. But right now, that potion's going to kill you if we don't fuck. We tried spells and waiting and all we got was a tentacle monster stringing me up in front of you like a new year's present. I'm not a religious woman. I don't even know if any gods are real now that I know Myva was a fake. But if they are, they're clearly trying to tell us something. Right now, it seems like they are telling us to cut to the chase. So let's get on with it."

"No, you're angry. You clearly don't want to."

"Listen," she sighed. "I can be annoyed and horny. If you're worried about my comfort, then don't. Sure we're strangers, but so far you've done all my chores for me and are apparently no stranger to commitment. I'm impressed, I'm intrigued, and I'm a little hot and bothered thanks to the tentacles. Not gonna lie, I've got at least three books with this exact same scenario. Except you're not a kraken-shifter and I haven't been sold to pay off my father's debts."

"What?"

"Felix, I'm giving you the go-ahead." Finally, she met my gaze. Brie lifted her chin and kept her voice firm. "But just so we're clear, this is strictly medicinal. I haven't agreed to be your wife. Should you feel differently when the curse has faded in two weeks, we can get an annulment at the courthouse and forget this whole thing. I won't hold anything against you."

There it was. The line in the sand. Perhaps it was easier for her to make it transactional. An out to protect both our emotions in case things go south. It was smart. But unacceptable. I've never been good with half measures. One way or another, I'd find my way into my little lamb's heart. The chase only added to the fun.

I moved closer, gripping her hips before brushing my lips against her thigh. "Does this mean I can do as I like then? For medicinal purposes, of course."

She shivered beneath my grip. "Yes."

One little word and my cock was throbbing painfully. It

would be all too easy to throw this chance away and just shove my tongue down her throat. Eat her cunt until all that mattered was the scent of her arousal on my tongue. Sink into her soft heat until I'd fucked away this ferocious need.

Breathe.

If this opportunity was going to work, then I needed to be smart. "Sweetheart, tell me what happened when the woman was sold to the Kraken." I let one of the shadow tendrils brush over her nipple, while two more wrapped around her ankles, spreading her legs wider.

"Why?" she whispered, tilting her head.

"I want to fulfill any of those fantasies while we have the chance." My fingers slid past her shoulders, guiding the robe down her arms before calling the tentacles to toss it away.

"This is supposed to be about you," she murmured.

I tilted her chin to look at me. "Make no mistake, Lamb, this is for me." She gasped as another tendril slid roughly against her pussy.

"Just like this wet cunt is for me. If I'm only allowed to have you until this curse ends, then I'm going to make the most of it. I want to know what it's going to take to get your nails digging into my back. I want you so needy for me that you bend over and show me that beautiful plump ass whenever I tell you to."

Her breath sped up, and her eyes darkened into the color of roasted chestnuts. Soft and rich, a decadent treat reserved for only the harshest of winter nights.

"You can tell me now, or I can guess," I said, pressing my lips against her throat, then letting a soft tendril of shadow wrap around it. Applying just enough pressure to assure her she wasn't going anywhere. "Would you like that? Did your Kraken take you gentle and slow?"

I trailed slow, deliberate kisses down her chest. Flicking my tongue over her nipple, then continued lower. She quivered beneath me as I called the tentacles to continue to play with her lavish body. "Or was he a feral beast?"

Her voice stammered as she answered. "Something like that."

Brie cried out when two of the limbs wrapped around each of her breasts and squeezed, while a smaller one gave a light slap to her ass. "Did he dream of licking your cunt the way I do?"

"I...Did you really dream of that?"

"Of course I did, sweetheart." I chased kisses down her lower belly and ran my thumb over her wet slit until she panted and jerked, trying to force the digit in. "Any man would drop to his knees and beg for the chance to eat you."

She laughed and rolled her eyes. "Any man under a love spell, you mean? I don't—AH!" Further protests were cut off when I shoved a finger inside her.

Wet juices from her cunt spilled onto my hand, making my mouth water.

The tentacle around her neck squeezed tighter in warning.

She made an annoyed noise but hushed at my stern look. "Lamb, we've agreed to do as I like to, remember? If I say I want to kneel down and worship this cunt, I will, and you won't question it. Understand?"

To emphasize my point, I sat back on my heels and arranged for her to be spread out on her back in front of me. Three large tentacles wrapped around her torso and ass to support her weight. With a wave of my hand, a smaller set of tendrils wove their way up her legs before spreading her lower lips for my view.

Oh, fuck yes. That pouting little flower was dripping.

I leaned in, inhaling her scent, before giving a long lick down the slit. She let out a little gasp and tried to wiggle forward, but I pulled away. "Answer me, Lamb."

"Yes," she said with a gasp. Her voice pitching into a whine when I let a limb press against her asshole.

"Good. Let me look at you now. You've been all I can think about since I first saw you. I haven't slept since."

"Wait, what? You need to sleep."

Unable to stop touching her, I let my hands roam the expanse of the thighs around my head. "I will," I said against her delicate skin. "We'll both be due for a long night's sleep after I've fucked this obsession for you out of me." My cock throbbed painfully when I felt her belly tighten. "Or maybe it won't be enough, and I'll have to keep you screaming well into the morning. We'll play it by ear," I said, taking my time to look at her.

Bondage wasn't something I'd tried in the past, but its merits became quickly known. With Brie completely under control like this, I could spread her anyway I liked until every curve was burned into memory. She was all mine. Mine to tease and fuck and sweet magic mishaps it felt so intoxicating. Enveloping and warm, like stepping into a hot spring after you've been frozen to the bone.

I closed my eyes, trying to savor the moment as long as possible. Then opened them to see Brie's parted lips. She panted as she watched me between her legs, her eyes molten pools of lust. It damn near broke me.

"Please. Please tell me if you need me to stop." At her nod, I bent down and buried my tongue in her cunt. Groaning at the taste of her, then traced around the little bud just above her entrance. In the guide book Isaak found, it mentioned a bundle of nerves called a clit that could render a woman into a simpering mess. When I sucked it, she let out some strangled half-panicked cry, before digging her heels into my shoulder blades, pushing me further against her.

We'll need to find that merchant and give him a generous tip.

As if the magic controlling the limbs heard my thoughts, the head of a smaller tendril split open, revealing a soft sucker. I concentrated on the shapes making up the shadow tendrils, testing out the ability to change their size and shape. *Well, that is just fucking brilliant.*

Brie whimpered and bit her lip. As if she was still worried

whether it was alright to enjoy this. I could feel her fighting to keep still as her mind raced. But quiet whimpers broke into sobs when I let the tentacles grow bolder. One dipping its tip into her ass while another replaced my tongue on her clit. *I won't let you feel guilty. You'll see just how much I'm enjoying this.* "Gods, you smell so fucking good."

She squeaked and jolted when I buried my nose against her folds, tonguing her deep. She tasted even better. Sweet and sultry, like a mermaid singing her irresistible melody, and I was a hapless sailor, all too willing to jump into the arms of death.

Fuck, it was too much. My cock was near weeping. A small bit of pre-cum dripped from the tip. I growled into her and wrapped a tentacle around the head. Forcing away all thoughts of an orgasm. I'll be damned if I come anywhere but buried in her slick cunt.

I leaned back, catching my breath. I placed a hand on her ass, letting my fingers sink into the soft skin, then sent a thicker tentacle to fuck her cunt. Gently at first. But the need to hear her cry out became unbearable when I saw the way she clenched down on the intruding limb. Gods, she'll be so tight around my cock. The thought of sinking into her, stretching that unbearable heat until I was buried to the hilt. She'd need to work up to being able to take my knot. Which was fine. I can be a patient man. Probably.

The tentacle around my cock tightened and stroked it.

Mimicking the desires I was too spellbound to will away. I watched her eyes flutter closed, teeth sink into the plump flesh of her lower lip. My pace increased and I let the tentacle in her ass push deeper, fucking her with slow deep strokes as the smaller tendril around her clit surrendered its slow pace and began to suck on her in earnest. My lamb's mouth fell open on a gasp before her eyes rolled to the back of her head.

"Felix," she screamed, her body quivering.

"Gods yes. Cry for me, gorgeous." Eager to try more of the book's teachings, I wrapped a tentacle around her stomach, let the bulbed end push down on her lower tummy as I worked her faster. Searching for that sweet spot just inside.

She curled into herself as her legs began to shake. "It feels so good," she sobbed. Brie thrust back against the tentacles inside her, and I curved the one in her cunt up just slightly to better hit her sweet spot. "Felix, oh gods, I'm gonna come."

The enraged look on her face when I removed the limb was priceless. She shook her head, trying to form words. "I... What?"

"Relax, we're just moving." Brie huffed out a breath but didn't protest when the tendrils lifted her upright. I lay down on my back and brought her to sit on my face. She braced herself above me, hovering her cunt just out of reach. "Sit down, love," I ordered.

She lowered herself a little more, then yelped when I smacked her ass. "I said sit."

"I'm heavy," she scolded. "Do you enjoy suffocating? Cause this is how you suffocate."

"Woman, if you don't sit down and come on my tongue—"

"I'm low enough, you can reach it—" The rest of her argument was lost in a sea of jumbled cries. I guess it's hard to argue with a suction cup against her clit. Brie let out a stream of desperate curses when I drove two tentacles back inside her. Working her body to the brink until her knees shook and gave out. I grabbed her ass and sat her down, letting my mouth join in the fun. She rocked against my face, unable to contain her composure any longer.

"Oh," she panted. "Oh, Felix, don't stop."

I lapped at her clit while keeping a steady, alternating pace between the tentacles in her cunt and ass. Then willed the one working her pussy to grow wider at the tip, with bumps running along the sides.

Her voice broke out into a keening whine, and I took the opportunity to suck hard on the jewel of her clit like a man possessed. My reward came in the form of dull nails digging into my shoulders. Brie's pink little pussy quivered as her body seized up, the muscles on her thighs going rigid. My sweet lamb choked out a wail and ground down further against me.

When the rolling waves of pleasure hit her, it was my name on her lips. A breathtaking sonata that rolled in thoughts of her and me, us, together in harmony. Sweet music dancing through days of joy and sorrow, savoring each touch and smile until the day we grew silent together. The satisfaction of such a life sent me over the edge. And despite my best efforts, I came hard, spilling my release on her back. I kissed her clit, ignoring the tinge of regret. This wouldn't be the last time we were together. Not even close.

My body hummed with sated pleasure and the power of the botched spell began to fade from my mind's grip. I let it go, watching the black tendrils fade into nothingness. Brie shuddered above me, then rolled to settle at my side. We lay there for a moment, breathing hard.

My hand found its way to her cheek, tracing the heart-shaped line of her jaw. Not bothering to resist the temptation, I moved on top of her, kissing her temple and running my fingers over the tight ringlets of her black hair. She giggled and wrapped her arms around my neck. This time, there was no reluctance from her. My lamb pulled me to her, brushing her soft lips over my own, before spreading her legs for me to settle in between. It didn't take long for my cock to rise at the invitation.

"Is this still alright?" I asked in between feathered kisses.

Brie's eyes were hooded, her long lashes casting shadows on her cheeks. "If it wasn't, I'd kick you off."

"Such a fierce little thing." I pressed my lips to hers again and pushed into her. Groaning into her throat as her body stretched to accommodate me, and she dragged her nails gently along my back, stroking and petting as I sank into her, inch by inch. I pulled her tighter against me, basking in the sensation, and moved my hips in shallow thrusts.

A moan vibrated in her chest, and she tightened her legs around me. When she pulled me in for a kiss, I thought I might die. Welcoming her sleek tongue against my own with unabashed eagerness. She made an inaudible sound of surprise when the base of my cock swelled inside of her. I held the back of her neck and soothed her with sweet words and soft caresses. Her brown eyes widened as I ground my cock to the bottom of her well. Her breath hitched, and she opened her legs wider, pulling at my waist to urge me onward. I could deny her nothing.

Braced on my elbow to keep from crushing her, I fucked her slow and deep, grinding my cock against the ring of muscles at the end of her cunt. Her breasts cushioned my chest as we moved together, neither in a hurry to finish. At least for today, we had all the time in the world.

She bit her lip as the knot at the base of my cock swelled further. "Felix, what is that?"

I eased my movements and ran my lips along her neck. "It's a knot, Lamb. Most shifters have them. Do you dislike it?"

Brie shook her head, a crease forming in her brow. "I like it…it's just…" Her eyes fluttered open, watery tears threatening to spill. "It's a little more intense than I expected."

"Do you need me to stop?"

"Opposite." Her hands dug into my back with primal need. "Please, move faster."

My eyes widened, and I sank my head into her shoulder, growling as I obeyed her demand, deep thrusts working inside her. Her body shook with new tremors. She continued to mewl, clawing at my back until she shouted out, hot tears streaming down her face.

As her climax took her, her legs quivered around me. I bared my fangs, my own release trying to chase after hers. I gripped her tighter, burying my nose in the scent of her hair, breathing deep as my shaft pulsed violently.

She pressed her nails into the sinew of my shoulders, pleading with me to come inside her. My knot swelled to its full size and it became damn near impossible to remove myself. Instead of thrusting, I ground deep inside her, rocking our bodies together in a frantic rhythm. I moaned and shuddered, my breath hissing through clenched teeth, and I emptied myself all over again. I rocked harder, digging my fingers into her hip as I came, murmuring her name.

When I finally collapsed against her, she ran her hand through my hair, caressing it away from my face. I rolled us to one side and pressed my forehead against hers. Feeling content and boneless as we lay in each other's arms.

In the dim light of the afternoon sun, Brie's skin glowed an almost bluish hue. Illuminated by a light sheen of sweat and contentment. It reminded me of countless days spent back home watching Ro paint. The elder orc would spend days in his study, crushing gems into fresh paint and crafting masterpieces out of thin air. People from all over Volsog would come to him asking for portraits and murals. When his hands became too old and pained to crush the gems into powder, he'd enlisted my services. Said it was payment for letting me dally around his study all the time. It was a job I took happily. No matter how hard he tried to teach me, I had no talent for painting. But it felt good to be a part of his process.

He told me once that the proper way to bring out the light in the people he painted was to never pick just one color similar to their skin tone. But instead, layer different hues of paint over each other. Each swipe of a new color brings out something new in the ones before. I didn't understand him then. Even as I watched him, I couldn't wrap my mind around how he was able to create such detailed works out of seemingly randomly selected colors. But looking at her now, I could see it. He'd start out with a deep lapis blue, then move on to shades of red and oranges, then back to lighter shades of blue. Blending them together until they formed something magnificent out of nothing.

I wished he was still around to paint her for me. Lapis blue was by far the hardest color to make. Each time he'd ask for it, I'd spend the day griping. But every time, he'd simply smile and tell me it was worth it. "You can't skimp out if you want something perfect." As usual, he was right. Some things were just worth the effort.

Chapter 6

Brie

Well, that did not go as planned. Felix squeezed me tighter to him, twitching in his sleep. I squinted, but the dark of the night left me mostly blind. Carefully, I untangled myself from his arms and slid off the bed. My fingers traced the edge of my nightstand until they brushed against the lantern I kept for midnight-snack guidance. Once lit, the room was filled with just enough light to move around comfortably.

It didn't matter how late in the night it was, there was no way I'd be able to fall back asleep. My mind was far too jumbled with terrible things, like emotions. I slipped on a plain green chemise, made my way downstairs and slid out the door into fresh air. The cool wood of my porch against my bare feet acted as an anchor back into reality.

"OK. So. That was probably a mistake," I said to the night. Felix wasn't just different dick. That was...I wasn't even sure what that was. But I wasn't sure how I was supposed to function in polite society after.

I took a deep breath and rested my hand on my knee. "Fuck."

That was amazing. My body still tingled from the places he touched. So everywhere, basically. I tingled everywhere, and it was making me think of stupid things, like taking him up on his offer to spend the day together in a flower field or going back to bed and asking him to do it again. "Damn it Brie, get a hold of yourself." The porch creaked as I paced its length. "You're just a little dickmatized. It happens. You can still keep your head about this."

But my mind was a backstabbing beast, and it flooded with images of Felix's soft whispers, his gentle hands as they worked another orgasm out of me after we woke up on the floor of my living room. Or how I screamed out his name as he took me bent over my bed, his hand fisted in my hair, growling salacious quotes from "Rejected Princess."

When did he even read it?

Normally, I'd never let a man grab my hair during sex. It just wasn't worth the work of re-doing the twists in the morning. But damn if Felix didn't make the effort worth my while. I pinched the bridge of my nose, trying to wrest the memory away. It didn't matter. It was just sex and I couldn't afford to let myself get swept up by him. I still had no way of knowing how much of his behavior was being dictated by the love potion. I growled and paced faster. That stupid bottle of pink disaster was messing up my whole life. Anything Felix did could be a complete lie. It would be stupid to let myself grow attached to someone whose feelings could evaporate in a week or so. If I wound up broken-hearted at the end of this, Jack was getting a foot to the throat.

Goosebumps raced along my arms, and I shivered. My stomach was in knots, twisting tighter every time I tried to bury down the butterflies dancing in the shape of the man in my bed. "I need to talk this over with someone." Cin's home was close by. But the little turd just got married, and I wasn't sure how her fire-breathing husband would react to being woken in the middle of the night.

Fucking Cin. Getting married right before I have an existential crisis.

Kitty was the only other friend I was close enough to wake up in the middle of the night, but she lived down by the ocean, and that was an hour's walk at best. A quick jaunt if I took my horse, but Chronic was an ornery beast if he didn't get his beauty sleep. I rubbed my temples in frustration. "You know what? I'm going to Cin's. I knew her first, and Fallon will just have to learn to sleep through our bullshit." We'd been having impromptu sleepovers since we were little. There was no rule that said we had to stop now.

Mind made up, I donned boots and stomped my way down the road. I had a bone to pick with her, anyway. She should have warned me these demons were a different breed.

It didn't take long for the winding oaks to fade into cinnamon trees. The comforting spicy smell eased my nerves a little. Rows and rows of pepper plants weaved their way in between the precious trees. They acted as a natural barrier to most vermin, so she made a point of spreading them around her farm. I still remember hiding in between cinnamon trees as we watched a young deer make the grave mistake of trying a ripe bright red cayenne. The poor thing reared back so fast we thought it might break its neck. It didn't come back after that.

I sucked in a breath and made my way up the hill where her cottage sat, but when I stepped past her nameplate, a wave of purple shimmered its way up a dome-like shape before coming to a stop just above her house. The strange light doubled back out, showing a massive barrier surrounding the property. I turned around to see the bottom of the barrier crackling angrily along the floor. I stepped back, almost stumbling over to avoid touching the strange magic. My back hit something hard, and I whipped around to see Fallon. The dragon shifter grabbed my shoulder to steady me before covering a yawn.

He gave a slow blink, as if trying to stay awake. "Brie, I didn't expect you. Is something wrong?"

"I...What is that?" I said, pointing to the fading shimmer.

"It's an alert barrier. Hold out your hand, I'll attune it to your energy so it won't go off if you enter the property."

Hesitantly, I raised my hand to him. Quicker than my eyes could track, he pricked the tip of my pointer finger with a needle. A small drop of blood rose. Fallon took my hand in his and held it above my head. He took a deep breath, then exhaled. I watched on in fascination as a plume of purple and black smoke spread down from the invisible dome and sucked up the small drop. The red of my blood blending into the swirling smoke, before it receded back into the barrier.

"There," he sighed, releasing my hand. "Now you can come and go without setting it off."

I rubbed at my wrist. "Oh, um. Thanks?"

He nodded and began walking back to the house. With his back turned, I finally noticed the intricate braid patterns tying back some of his long hair. They came together in a spiral knot at the back of his head, while the rest of his hair fell freely below it. No doubt because of his wife's handiwork after his little conniption about shaving. "I assume you're here for Cin? She's most likely woken up by now. I'll put on some tea."

"Thank you," I murmured, following behind him. Looks like he's not a grumpy sleeper. That's good news. "Sorry to drop by so late."

"It's fine," he shrugged. "Cin warned me that unexpected drop-ins are common here. So the magic has already been attuned to her family, and now you."

I hummed and followed him inside. Cin made her way downstairs and greeted me with a tired wave, then snatched two bottles of wine and promptly threw herself onto the couch, her long, flowing pink nightdress billowing dramatically around her, before landing in an ungraceful slump around her calves. She held up one bottle and swirled its contents. I took it greedily and slumped into my chair.

Fallon peered in from the kitchen. "No tea then? Perfect, I'm going back to bed," he said, not waiting for an answer. He retreated back up the stairs, ducking his head to avoid his horns scraping the ceiling. "If you need me, don't," he called down.

Cin rolled to her side, bit the cork from her wine bottle, and spit it out. She took a long sip and sat up to look me over. My friend rested a hand on her cheek, before a slow crooked grin spread across her face. "He blew your back out, didn't he?"

I let out an aggravated breath and uncorked my own wine. "You should have warned me," I hissed.

She threw back her head and laughed, damn near rolling off the couch in her fit. "My love!" she shouted at the ceiling. "I won the bet!"

A loud thud sounded off from the room above.

"Damn it!" I grimaced and nursed my drink. "You two are the worst."

"I can't tell you how validating it is to see someone else go through this." Cin rubbed her hands together in glee. "Tell me everything," she said, giggling. "Did he live up to the were-wolves in your romance books?"

Heat rushed to my cheeks, and I looked back to the stairs to make sure Fallon hadn't come back down before answering. "He said, 'I see your book wolves and I raise you tentacle play.' "

Cin's eyes widened to the size of dinner plates. "No!?"

"Yes," I whispered back. "Cin, I'm trying to be calm and collected about this entire ordeal but that man is making me—" I tried to find the right words, but instead just fluttered my arm around like my thoughts would arrange themselves better through interpretive jazz hands. "I'm not OK, alright? I'm alarmed."

Cin adjusted her matching pink bonnet and settled in deeper in her seat. "Emotional, confused, questioning your moral compass and whether or not you had one in the first place?" she asked.

I pointed my drink at her and slapped my hand on the soft cushioning of her love seat. "Yes, that exactly."

She pumped her fists in the air and wiggled around in her seat. "This is great. I'm so happy you have a mate, too."

Guilt reared its ugly head in the pit of my stomach. "That's the issue," I began. "We only slept together because it looked like the effects of the love potion were about to give him a heart attack. I've got no right getting excited over a man who's forced to find me interesting. The original plan was to keep it as a quickie and be done with it. But..."

"But?" she pressed.

I winced and looked away. "Um...The man makes a compelling case for longer sessions. Let's just leave it at that. Either way, it doesn't change the fact that his feelings could change at the drop of a hat when this is over. He may think he's imprinted, but it's best I keep him at a distance while there's no guarantee."

"But you already like him," Cin said. It wasn't a question. She knew me better than that.

I nodded.

She hummed. "Then are you really saving yourself any trouble by still fighting it?"

"What do you mean?"

"I know you, Brie," she said, "You've got more walls than a kingdom under siege. Any time a man shows up that you take a fancy to, you find something wrong with him and end things before you get too attached."

"No, I don't," I snapped.

She raised an eyebrow. "You broke your last suitor's heart because you, oh what was it?" she said, tilting her head to the side. "Oh, that's right, because he ate tomatoes weird," she said, fixing me with a glare.

I sputtered around my drink. "Who eats a whole tomato with a spoon? Just bite it! That's a perfectly valid reason to end a relationship."

She pointed a finger at me, her eyes narrow. "You're scared

of commitment and everyone on this side of Kinnamo knows it. Except this time you can't run away. Be it an imprint or love potion, Felix isn't gonna take your bullshit excuses. You can continue to fight this on the grounds of moral hierarchy, but that ship has sailed. You've already slept together and from the looks of it, he's already gotten under your skin. Hell, there's still a chance he'll drop dead if you were to stop sleeping with him at this point, so would it really be such a bad thing to see where this goes?"

Frustration bubbled in my throat, making my words come in angry hisses. "And what happens if he loses interest and leaves me in the lurch after this?"

"Then you get hurt," she said simply. "You get hurt. We begin the ceremonial break-up binge and we move on."

"Well, of course it all sounds so easy when you say it like that," I grumbled into my wine.

Cin rolled her eyes and took a swig of her drink. "Only because I know how impossible you're trying to make it sound in your head."

"Maybe I should have made the trek to Kitty's house after all."

Cin paused. "Brie, Kitty is one of the girls that went missing today."

My heart jumped in my throat at her words. "What?"

She sat up straighter in her chair. "I assumed Felix told you."

"He mentioned a few girls went missing but didn't say who," I said. Chills ran down my spine and my mind started to race. I'd been so wrapped up in my own shit that I didn't even think to ask who went missing.

"Now don't panic just yet," Cin said, holding a hand up. "They've been gone less than a day. It's possible they all just went on a getaway and didn't tell anyone. Kitty, Serena, and Willow always run in a group. It wouldn't be the first time they'd gone off together."

"But why wouldn't they tell anyone?"

"I don't know," she said solemnly. "But tomorrow Fallon and I are going to resume the search party, just in case. If you can convince Felix to join the hunt too, that would be great. Werewolves are known trackers."

I nodded and tried to find comfort in her plan. But my hands shook around the bottle of wine. "He said he couldn't find any trace."

"Any trace in the village," she began. "First thing in the morning, we'll start sweeping the surrounding area in groups. Fallon, Dante and I will be in the air, so we can cover a wider range. Between that and the groups searching the ground, we're bound to find something. Knowing my cousin, she probably convinced the other two to go bar hopping in Panshaw at the last minute. You know how Kitty gets."

I stared at her. "Did you mean how you *both* get?"

Cin sniffed and took another long drink.

"The irony of you two being the same person and yet hating each other will never be lost on me."

"Yeah, well, that's how I know she's fine." She raised her glass and made a hair flip motion which didn't quite work as well with her long curls tied up in the bonnet. "We Hotpeppers are tough like that."

Tension eased its way out of my shoulders as I focused on taking deep calming breaths. "Yeah. I'm sure they're alright."

I looked back at my friend, but her eyes had gone to some faraway place. The bottle in her hands was gripped so tightly her knuckles grew pale, and I mentally kicked myself for not seeing it sooner. The last time we did a village-wide sweep, it was for her sister. Days of searching turned into weeks, and we still found nothing. Tomorrow's search was going to eat her alive.

I reached over and squeezed her hand. "No one will blame you if you sit this one out."

She smiled and blinked away the tears forming in her eyes. "I'll blame myself if I don't. Besides, the more eyes we have in the sky, the better. Crash and Smash won't let anyone else ride them aside from myself and Chili, and you know that coward won't trust a flying horse."

I wouldn't trust a flying horse. Chili was always the practical one of the 'Pepper siblings. If death by a thousand-foot drop made him a coward, then call me chicken, as I was right there firmly on the ground with him. My bones creaked and popped as I got up, the events of the day finally taking their toll on my exhausted mind. "I'll let you go back to sleep. We'll need it for tomorrow."

Nodding, Cin rose and placed her bottle on the end table. "Are you going to be alright walking back by yourself? I can wake up Fallon, so we can come with you."

I shook my head. "It's just down the street. I'm sure I'll manage."

Cin walked me to the door as we bid our farewells. The night's chill was slightly less cutting with the help of wine in my belly, and I welcomed it with open arms.

"Brie," Cin called. I turned back to see her leaning against her door frame. The worry in her brow was gone, but I could still see the stress of tension lining her eyes. "I know the situation isn't ideal. But Felix is good people."

She glanced off in thought. "...Well, when he's not acting crazy. Just...don't be afraid to give him a chance, OK?"

The fact that he was good was the part I was struggling with. I wasn't one to get attached quickly in a relationship. Most times, I had to work my way up to even being able to accept physical forms of affection. But with him, it was just... different. And that was terrifying. It was easy to picture him as too good to be true with the threat of a love potion hanging over us. The heartbreak ending seemed inevitable. I'd never been lucky in relationships before, so I didn't see how this would be any different. "I'll try."

"Thanks," she sighed, before heading back inside.

I made my way back down the road, letting my mind wander. Maybe Cin was right. It's not like I had any intention of letting him die, so ignoring him wasn't an option. And Felix was sweet…a little crazy. But sweet. Besides, the search for the missing women was enough stress on everyone's mind.

There was no need to tack on the extra stress of my own insecurities. The search party would need to take priority, and I'd just have to roll with my man problems until we found them. I wouldn't be the first woman to let go of my inhibitions for a week or two.

"That's right," I said, clenching my fist. "Flings happen all the time. If I get hurt in the end, then I'll just pick up the pieces and start over. I'm a grown woman. I can handle this."

After taking a deep breath of the night air, I coughed up a rotten smell.

Putrid waves of death made my eyes water. Something must have curled up and died in the woods. Though it was odd, I didn't smell it on the way over. Whatever it was, it must have been dead for a while. I rubbed my nose on my sleeve and continued down the path. A chilly breeze nipped at my heels, swirling up leaves from the cobblestones before drifting off ahead of me as if the wind itself was trying to escape. I walked faster. The lean and sway of the old oak trees suddenly felt a little too ominous for my liking.

"Help," a feminine voice called out. Icy dread seeped deep into my bones at its call. I didn't look back to see what it was. There was something in its tone. An otherness that had me damn near ready to piss myself. Aside from me, there shouldn't have been anyone else out so late in the night. My only neighbors close by were Cinnamon and Jack. And that sure as shit wasn't Jack's voice.

I mentally tried to place how far away the voice was, and how long I could maintain a sprint. My cheesy-baked-potato-loving ass wasn't much for running, but I could do it in a pinch. Or at least try.

"Help me," the thing called again, sounding an awful lot like none of my business. I swallowed thickly, raising my lantern higher as I sped up. Branches creaked in the distance. The creature's voice rolled in a somber timbre. "Come back."

"Go fuck yourself," I muttered. Panic made the hairs on the back of my neck rise. Home was less than half a mile away. I just needed to maintain enough distance until then.

Behind me, I heard a tree branch break and a loud clop of hooves slapped loudly against the stone road.

"Come back," it groaned again. The rancid smell grew stronger, making me cough.

Nope. Nope. Nope. Not me, not tonight, not ever.

Its otherworldly voice lost its feminine edge. Replaced by a wail of several nightmares rolled into one. "Come back. Come back." The clopping noises sped up, accompanied by a high-pitched screech of struck stone. "COME BACK, COME BACK, COME BACK."

I screamed for help and ran for all I was worth. The haunting clop of its hooves grew closer, no matter how fast I tried to push myself. I blinked away tears and screamed for Felix. Hoping the werewolf's hearing would be strong enough to hear me this far away. A shadow flew over my head and landed with a thud a few feet in front of me. I skittered to a halt to avoid crashing into it. The dim light of the lantern flickered in the darkness, revealing the monster.

Its head was that of a deer's skull. It hunched forward, glowing yellow eyes peering at me from sunken sockets. When the light flickered brighter, I could just make out the twisted branches coming out the back of its neck. The creature stepped toward me on all fours, sharp claws ticking against the cobblestone. Its emaciated body rippled as it cocked its head to the side. Its bone mouth clacked together in quick succession with loud ticks. The creature's head turned up and down as if studying me. With a final clack, it reared up on two legs, the hooves of its back legs clicking loudly as it stumbled to support its own weight. "Felix," it screamed. "Felix, help me."

I stepped back in a panic. It continued screeching the words I just yelled, its high-pitched voice altering until it sounded just like mine. "What the fuck are you?" I asked.

The monster looked around us, screeching for Felix, using my voice before it turned to look at me. Its haunting gaze rooted me to the floor. It shook its head slowly, as if mocking me. "No help. No Felix."

Alright, the insult to injury seemed a little unnecessary.

It was bad enough I was about to get eaten by the spare parts of a depressed taxidermist's wet dream. It didn't need to toy with my emotions as well. The creature let out a sickly laugh and moved closer. Its putrid stench rolled off of it like a wave of armor. I inched backwards, my pulse beating in war drums in my ears.

The beast lunged, knocking the wind out of my lungs as I went down hard. I cried out and dropped my lantern when its claws dug into my arm. The glass shattered on the ground, releasing the flame in a sea of scattered dead leaves. Flickers of yellow and orange lapped at the loose foliage until the flame rose high enough to touch the monster's side. It screeched and reared up away from the flame, circled behind me and reached for my shoulder. I rolled out of the way and snatched the remains of the lantern, throwing it as hard as I could at its exposed skull.

The monster shielded its face, but its arm caught flame. Ear-shattering screams erupted as it tried to shake off the fire. I took my chance and bolted down the road. Clouds blocked the moon's light from view as I ran half-blind into the darkness. "COME BACK," it roared, still using my voice. "COME BACK, COME BACK."

"Why would I listen to you?" I screamed back. An enormous figure broke out of the trees down the road. I tried to stop and turn around, but slipped on wet leaves and barreled right into it. Without thinking, I lashed out, kicking and clawing at the mass of fur. *I'm not dying here, I won't do it!*

My efforts proved futile when a clawed hand pinned my wrists together. I shot up, trying to bite at its wrists, when I noticed the monster holding me captive wasn't even looking at me. Its red eyes fixated on the screaming mess of the deer beast charging towards us. When I squinted, I could just make out the color of familiar blond fur. "Oh sweet baby jaguars, you're Felix."

The werewolf didn't take his eyes off the flaming creature. "Lamb, don't look." He moved me behind him and stepped forward. I scrambled on wobbly knees and hid behind an oak tree.

"THAT'S MINE," the deer beast roared. I peered around from behind the tree to see it closing in on Felix. Its left arm was still smoking, but it charged ahead, screeching and screaming its head off. "THAT'S MINE. IT'S MINE, IT'S M—"

In retrospect, I probably should have heeded his warning not to look. I could admit fault on that one. Watching its jaw get smashed into the back of its skull was going to haunt me for a few years, at least. The deer monster's screeching turned to choked gurgles as it tried to slash Felix with its claws.

But the werewolf merely snatched its wrist and snapped it back. Blood shot out past exposed bone, and my stomach churned.

I watched on in horror, unable to look away as Felix tore into the beast. No matter how hard the deer beast fought, it was no match for the much larger werewolf. It wasn't even a fight. He just mauled the wretched thing beyond recognition.

Tearing into its chest and shredding it into blood-red ribbons. Finally, the monster below Felix grew still and quiet.

He stood, shaking the gore off his hands, before he turned back to me. The clouds had finally freed the moon, and gods, I wish they hadn't. In the pale glow of night, with the light yellow of his fur stained with unmistakable red, there was no denying what Felix was. It was easy to romanticize werewolves in the fairy tale romances that lined my bookshelves. But in person... in person, he just looked like a monster.

In the back of my mind, Fallon's voice kept repeating the ending to Kinnamo's creation story. There was a woman in my exact same position before, and she wound up dead. Killed by a werebear who couldn't handle the effects of a love potion.

My knees buckled under me. I tried to get my breathing under control, but panic grew with each step he took toward me. I pulled my knees to my chest and shielded my head with my arms. The sound of crunching leaves grew closer until I felt the heat of his body as he knelt down beside me.

The rough pad of his thumb gently grazed across my cheek, wiping tears away. "It's alright, Lamb. It's dead now."

I glanced up at him, but the sight of his glowing red eyes only made my fear grow. "I don't wanna die," I cried.

Felix's tone was soothing. Well, as soothing as a voice could be coming past a row of fangs. "You're not going to die, sweetheart. I'm here."

He tried to gather me in his arms, but I scrambled away.

His long ears dropped low, and he backed away from me. He sat down a little ways away and rested his head on his hand.

"Still scared of this form, eh?" he sighed, and closed his eyes. "I'll turn back as soon as I can. Right now I'm still too angry."

So he said, but when he opened his eyes again, Felix was smiling. His soft grin lighting up his wolfish features like he hadn't a care in the world.

"Y-you don't look angry," I sniffed.

He hummed and tilted his head. "What can I say, love? Being around you makes me smile."

A laugh broke out in between my tears. "That was so lame."

He grinned wider. "But it made you laugh." Felix moved a little closer, testing the waters. When I didn't flinch, he settled next to me on the ground. Close, but not enough to touch.

I wanted to be brave enough to close the distance. Reach out and take the comfort he was trying to give, but my body wouldn't budge. "Felix, I don't know if I can do this."

"Do what, Lamb?"

After wiping away my tears, I tried to keep my voice from stammering. "Being with you. I know you're not trying to scare me, but I can't stop thinking about the bear-shifter that killed the dragon's wife and I'm terrified you're going to snap and break my neck or something and—"

"Whoa, slow down," he said. "What bear-shifter? What's happened?"

I sniffed and recounted Kinnamo's creation story the best I could. Felix sat stone still, taking it all in. When I finished, he didn't speak. We sat together for a moment. The only sound was the rustle of leaves and my stupid sniffling. After a short while, Felix buried his head and his hands and sighed.

"Well. No fucking wonder you're terrified."

"Yeah, it's not the best creation story," I said.

"It's terrible is what it is," he snarled. His tail moved to curl around me, the soft fur tickling against my ankle. In a way, it was oddly comforting. Not every part of him in this form was made for killing. Just most of it. He let out a breath and stared up at the moon. "I'm not strong enough to stay away from you, Brie."

"I know," I said, wiping at my eyes again.

He grinned sheepishly at me. "At least I don't look like I'm crazy enough to kill you, right?"

I dropped my hand from my face and stared at him. "You are *covered* in blood."

He chuckled and looked away. "You're right. That was a dumb question."

"Do you know what that monster was?"

He nodded and opened his fist to reveal a small blue crystal. It pulsed with a low, faded light. "It was a ghoul. Most of them are malevolent spirits that feed on grave sites. But judging by the gem, this one was a familiar. The power gem gives it life, and it's normally hidden somewhere inside the body. You could cut a ghoul to pieces and the damn things still won't go down until you remove its power source."

"What's a familiar?" I asked.

"Servants to witches and mages. Normally, it's just a weak spirit that takes the form of a small animal. But this power gem tells me that our brittle friend didn't start out as a spirit. This was a human turned into a ghoul."

I shuddered and looked at the lump of remains. "That can happen?"

He nodded. "I've only heard tales of it done before. The magic required would normally be enough to kill a witch before she could complete the spell. The ghoul was after you. So I'd wager it also had something to do with our missing women problem."

My hands shook when I remembered the feminine voice the beast used when it tried to call me. It may have belonged to one of the women. "Did it eat them?"

"No," he began. "There was nothing in its stomach. Whatever its master wants with them, they most likely want them taken alive," Felix said, standing up. "I'll need to report this to Fallon, so he can try to trace its magic back to the source. Do you want me to escort you back home, or would you prefer not to see me for a while?"

I shot up and snatched his free arm. "You're not leaving me alone. I'm coming too," I said, squeezing his arm to my chest.

He looked down at me. "I thought you were too scared to be near me?"

"You're terrifying. We've established this. But you're also able to kill those things easily, so I'm staying with you." I peered into the darkness of the woods. Checking to see if any more ghouls would pop out from nowhere. The last thing I wanted was to be alone in my house. There could be more monsters waiting inside for all I knew.

Felix hung his head. "I see. Is that all I am to you, beloved? A guard dog?" he teased.

"No," I said, patting his thick bicep. "You're also a decent farmhand."

"Brat."

Chapter 7

Brie

Turns out Fallon saves his grumpiness for men. At least, that's how it seemed when he opened the door and immediately tried to set Felix on fire. I stood pressed against the wall of Cin's home as I watched the werewolf dodge an angry flurry of flaming fists. In werewolf form, Felix was a lot bigger than Fallon, but from where I was standing, the wolf man looked ready to run for his life.

Felix ducked his head to avoid another swing, but Fallon caught him in the side with a kick and sent him to the ground hard. Felix laughed and put his hands up in surrender. "Just wait, I have a good reason this time!"

"Bullshit," Fallon growled, before aiming another kick at

his head. "If you woke me up for another one of your stupid games, I'll shove Gorgonzola down your throat until you shit out your soul."

"I love you too," Felix crooned, which earned him another flaming swipe. He managed to roll out of the way before it singed his ear, then jumped up and backed away from the dragon shifter. "But I'm serious. We have a good reason to be here." He dusted himself off and turned to me. "Don't we, wife?"

"Oh, um yeah. Hold on." I dug the gem out of my pocket and held it up.

Cinnamon dragged herself out of the house and slumped against the door frame. Her pink bonnet was half off, letting the wild portion of curls poof out on one side. She blinked at the scrapping men, then turned her tired gaze to me. "He just called you wife."

Felix grinned wide and held his head up. "She didn't tell you? We got married yesterday."

I flinched and shot a glare at him. "Now is not the time!" I hissed.

He tilted his head, taking on an innocent tone. "But if not now, darling, when?"

"Yes, Brie," Cinnamon purred. The edge in her voice was practically a knife to my throat. "Best friend of twenty years, whom I just spoke to less than an hour ago. When were you going to tell me you were married?" she said, crossing her arms.

"It's not what it looks like. He just threatened the courthouse into giving him a marriage certificate. You know if I was having a real wedding, you'd be the first person I told," I said.

Cin tsked but relaxed her posture.

"She also took my name," Felix chirped.

I stomped my foot and swatted his direction. "Would you just stop it!"

Fallon shook the flames off his arms. They faded out into wisps of smoke before disappearing from his ruined shirt. "Do humans normally take on their husbands' names?" he asked Felix.

He nodded, a smug smile spread across his maw as he eyed Fallon. "It's how they combine families here. Most human marriages aren't recognized until they've registered at the courthouse and the couple has decided on which name to take. If not, then it's just considered shacking up, and the woman is still technically single."

The dragon shifter's mouth fell open in shock and turned to Cin.

She didn't bother looking at him. Cin kept her glare firmly aimed at me and held a hand up to Fallon. "Don't start with me right now. I've been betrayed."

This is getting out of hand. "I did not betray you. I didn't mention it because... well I forgot. It's been a long few days."

Felix clapped his hands to his cheeks in mock horror. "My love, how could you?"

Heat flooded my face, and I slammed my hand on the

railing of Cin's porch. "I will personally hand Fallon an entire wheel of cheese. Keep trying me."

He opened his mouth but snapped it shut when I swatted at him again. I pinched the bridge of my nose and let out a breath.

"Crystal," I grumbled. "I got attacked by a ghoul and Felix pulled this crystal out of its chest." The small gem flickered as I brought it up to show Fallon. "He said you might be able to use it to find the missing women."

Fallon took one look at the gem and nodded, then gave Felix a swift kick to the side. "Next time lead with that," he said.

The werewolf snickered and got to his feet. "You're so mean without your beauty sleep."

Fallon took the gem from me and inspected it closer. Black smoke rolled off his hands to surround it. Swirling around the crystal until every bit of blue was swallowed up. After a moment, the smoke faded and he let out a curse.

"What is it, hun?" Cin asked.

His brow scrunched together as he continued to turn the gem around in his hand. "The damn thing is warded up like a fortress. Whoever did this knew exactly what they were doing. It's going to take a few days at least to force my way around it."

"But you can, right?" I asked. "If that ghoul really took Kitty and the others, then we may not have a few days."

"I can. But judging by the strength and time put into this one gem, I'd say whoever is doing this isn't just looking to snatch a few women to kill for fun," he said, moving to sit on the steps of the porch. "If they're lucky, then they're being kept alive to be used as a power source."

"How are a bunch of women a power source?" Cin asked. "I don't think anyone in Boohail practices magic."

"It's not them specifically. Every human has large, natural magic reserves. Most creatures are bound by a certain type of magic. For fox-shifters it is nature, for dragons it's elemental based. With proper training, you might be able to do a few spells outside of your base magic type, but it's incredibly diffi-cult. The only reason I can is because I absorbed Myva's magic. But humans don't have that restriction. Your magic can do a wide range of spells because you have no magic type. The only caveat is that most humans cannot tap into it. That being said, it's all too easy for an ambitious witch to use humans as fodder for more powerful spells."

"You say that like it's happened before," Cin said.

"It has," he replied. "You used to call her Goddess."

"Myva was taking our magic?" Cin asked.

He sighed and ran a hand through his hair. "You probably didn't even realize it was happening. With so many humans coming in and out of her temples leaving offerings and prayers, she'd been able to sip off your magic reserves with no one feel-ing any different." Fallon's jaw tightened as he rolled more black smoke over the gem. "This is deeply concerning. What-ever spell they're trying to cast can't be good."

"What do we do?" Felix asked.

The dragon shifter pocketed the gem and stood. "Have any males been taken that we know of?"

Felix shook his head. "Last I checked, it was just the three women."

"Does it matter if they're just taking women?" I asked.

"Possibly. It could just be that our kidnapper has a type. Either way, we'll need to put out a village-wide curfew. Ghouls are weak to sunlight, so it's unlikely that anyone will be taken in daylight." He turned to his wife. "Rabbit, send a pigeon out to as many houses as you can, instructing women not to go out at night. Then send one to the ship and tell Usha to have the men set up a night patrol around the village."

Cinnamon plucked nervously at a loose string on her sleeve. "What about the search party? We can't just forget about the women they've already taken."

He put a hand on her shoulder and squeezed. "We're not, I promise you. But there's no point in sending out valuable fighters on a wild goose chase if I can find out their location using the gem. As soon as I've cracked its protection wards, we can attack in full force."

I shifted on my feet, worry churning in my gut. "Is the kidnapper really that dangerous? I mean, you're a dragon. They can't pose much of a threat to you."

His expression didn't give me much reassurance. "If we were dealing with any kind of demon or monster, then I wouldn't worry. But right now, we do not know what kind of magical threat we're dealing with. Going in blind could spell disaster for everyone involved."

"Oh." I stared down at my feet, trying to fight off the growing panic. "Right, that makes sense." *If a fucking dragon is worried about whatever this thing is, then what chance do the rest of us have?*

Felix came to my side and rested a massive clawed hand on the small of my back. "We're just being cautious, Lamb. Whoever is doing this doesn't stand a chance once we smoke them out of their hole. Then tall, dark and angry will take care of them easily. Won't you, Fallon?" he asked.

The dragon shifter's demeanor shifted into loosely concealed rage. Gold swirled in his dark eyes and blue and black sparks danced in the smoke licking at his ankles. "Whatever cretin that has been poaching in my territory will wish they simply threw themselves into a pit of spikes. Once my humans are out of the way, I'll erase the perpetrator's entire family line from existence."

An icy shiver ran down my spine at his words. "His humans?" I whispered to Felix.

He ducked low, and the soft fur on his face brushed against my temple when he answered. "It's a dragon thing. Anything in Boohail is considered part of his hoard."

I glanced at Cin, but my friend looked completely unfazed by Fallon's behavior. Instead, she slipped on a pair of sandals and headed to her pigeon coop without a word.

She paused and turned back to me. "Brie? He's not joking. Don't go outside at night unless you have to. I know how much you love your night walks."

"As if I'm ever going out at night again after dealing with that crazy deer thing," I said.

She smiled and nodded. "Good." With that, she turned and ran to the coop.

Felix patted my back. "Let's leave Fallon to his work, love."

I nodded and turned to say my goodbyes, but Fallon had engulfed himself in a shroud of smoke. The swirling mass grew larger and spilled off the deck into the grass. All at once, the shroud shot up, forming into a massive black dragon. Its long body weaved around fields of spices, blowing up cinnamon-smelling dust until he coiled into himself. Clawed hands rose in front of him, and his dark magic held up the small crystal. His brow furrowed and the long black whiskers on his snout swayed behind his head in a smooth, rhythmic pattern.

Too stunned to move, Felix guided me down the steps and we made our way towards home. "Are you doing alright, Lamb?" he asked.

I shook my head and tried to gather my thoughts. "Can we go back to the 'his humans' thing? Are we supposed to pay taxes to him or something?" *That is one debt collector I never want to cross.*

Felix barked out a laugh. "No. Dragons are just a possessive lot. I don't think I ever saw the stone dragon that ruled over my homeland. But if there was ever a giant rampaging cretin or other outside threat, it was usually dead before any of us had to deal with it. Some dragon lords are more involved than others, but most will just mind their business until something they consider a threat messes with their territory."

A lump formed in my throat. "Are...are rampaging Kraken common?"

He hummed and tilted his hand back and forth. "Occasionally. Who knows what sets off those overgrown squids."

Great. Awesome. First deer ghouls, a crazy kidnapper, and now Kraken.

Wonderful, just bring on all the magical murderers. Why the fuck not?

I kept my focus on the road in front of me, just trying to put one foot in front of the other. So engrossed in my mission not to trip over my own feet, I didn't even notice when Felix stopped at my front door. My forehead slammed against the hardwood, finally knocking me out of my stupor.

Felix covered his snout, trying to hide his laughter. "Normally we have to open doors first, sweetheart."

My face heated, and my hands fumbled around the doorknob. "I know that," I grumbled, swinging the door open.

"Of course," he said. "I'll see you in the morning. Try to get some sleep."

Anxiety set my nerves on edge when he turned to leave. I snatched his arm and held it tight. "Wait, where are you going?"

The werewolf grinned and patted the hand holding him hostage. "I'm just going to wash myself off and sleep in the barn. I'll be able to hear you if anything should go bump in the night."

"Well, what if whatever's bumping has already killed me by the time you get over here?" My voice squeaked, but I was too scared to care.

He raised a brow at me. "You know I'd love nothing more than to sleep with you if you've suddenly lost your fear of me."

Felix's words made me pause. The deer creature was beyond terrifying, but he was the one that ripped it to shreds like it was nothing. My gut twisted into knots and I started to sweat. He didn't look like a complete madman yet, but it was possible the bear-shifter didn't lose it right away, either.

At my hesitation, he gave my hand a comforting squeeze and turned to leave. Before he could make it off the front steps of the porch, I darted in front of him and held my arms out, blocking his path.

"Th-the couch!" I stammered.

Felix's large frame towered over me. The sharp daggers of his fangs poked past the top of his snout and the haunting red eyes of a predator were a little more than intimidating. He could gut me like a fish if he was so inclined. Yet his hands were gentle when he guided me home. Even now, with all my indecisiveness, the werewolf was just waiting patiently for me to tell him what I wanted. Cinnamon said he was good people. I trusted her more than anyone. And if I was being fully honest, I was a lot more scared of another ghoul showing up than him. As foolish as that might have been.

My knees shook when I tried to look him in the eye, but I did my best to stomp down my nervousness. "Can you sleep on the couch? In human form, I mean."

He tilted his head to the side and watched me for a moment. "You'll be alright with me so close?"

"Probably?" I shrugged. "You haven't hurt me yet, but a ghoul already has. I'm not going to lie and say I'm not scared of you, but I think I'd feel safer if you were closer."

A low thumping sound knocked against the porch railing, but it was too dark to see what it was. "Alright," he said.

"Is your tail wagging?" I asked.

"No." The thumping stopped.

He is strangely adorable for a monster. I let out a sigh of relief and clapped my hands together. "Great, I'll get you some blankets."

I made my way back inside, then paused when I noticed he wasn't following. Instead, Felix made his way further into the dark night. "Wait, where are you going?"

He turned back and held up his hands. "I'm still filthy, remember? Something tells me you wouldn't appreciate blood on your nice upholstery." My fingers clenched the door frame tight. I peeked back into my pitch black house, half expecting some monstrosity to pop out as soon as he got far enough away.

"Oh, right. Make it quick, OK?" I asked. The amount of fear

in my voice was embarrassing. But pride could go fuck itself when compared to monsters in the dark.

Felix grinned, the white of his fangs standing out against the darkness. "Anything for you, Lamb."

With that, I set to work setting up the couch for a good night's rest. Well, after stubbing my toe a few times, fumbling around trying to find my extra lantern. Night-time was overrated. I shook out the spare blankets and sneezed when a thin layer of dust kicked up. It must have been longer than I thought since I last had company spend the night. I took out my frustration on the intruding dust bunnies and laid out the makeshift bed. Once the pillows were sufficiently fluffed, and the lavender incense was replaced with a fresh stick, I took a step back and rested a hand on my hip. *This will do. Just because I'm a coward doesn't mean I have to be a poor host.*

The marriage certificate sitting on the coffee table caught my eye. My name was hastily scribbled next to Felix's. Most likely done by whatever terrified clerk he managed to rope into his shenanigans. *Is it still considered hosting if he's sort of my husband?*

My ruminations were interrupted by the sound of the front door opening.

I turned to greet my sort of husband, only to shield my eyes at his nudity. "Cheese and rice, cover up!" I demanded. I could feel the man's smug look without even seeing him. But I sneaked a peek through my fingers. I'm only human.

"That wasn't what you were saying a few hours ago, love." He moved through the room and took a throw blanket from the love seat and wrapped it around his waist.

"Times change," I said, dropping my hands.

He settled himself into the nest of blankets and patted at the space next to him. "Would you like to join me now, or should I wait until you undoubtedly hear something scurrying outside?"

I narrowed my eyes at him and crossed my arms. "I'm sure I'll manage fine in my own bed."

"Of course, Lamb. I'm sure nothing has managed to hide itself upstairs yet. You'll be fine."

A prick of fear raced down my spine, and I looked to the staircase. "What? Why would you say that?"

His voice took on an innocent tone. "I said you'll be fine." He placed his hands behind his head and closed his eyes. "Well, goodnight, darling. Say hello to the Hungry Man for me."

"Nice try, jerk," I said, throwing a pillow at his head. "Cin told me all about your Hungry Man and it won't work on me."

"Pity," he sighed.

I held my chin up and snatched the lantern off the table. Its dim light flickered against the room's objects, casting sinister shadows I refused to acknowledge. With as much false confidence as I could muster, I headed upstairs to bed.

Chapter 8

Felix

Endless darkness surrounded me on all sides. I reached out my arms, trying to find something to touch. But there was nothing there.

There never was. No sound. No smell. No light. Just nothing. I tried to scream, desperate to hear the sound of my own voice, but that didn't work either. It didn't matter how much I fought; the result was always nothing.

I didn't know how long I was floating in the abyss, but it felt like an eternity. Focusing all of my attention on my ears, I tried to listen for any sound. Any scratch or call that would pull me away from this miserable darkness.

It wasn't the first time I was trapped in the dark. That much

I knew. But for the life of me, I couldn't remember how I got out last time. *I think there was a smell. Dammit all, what was it?* Whatever it was, there was no trace of it here.

Frustrated and scared, I lashed out into the nothingness. *I hate this. Somebody please get me out. I can't remember how to get out.* My lips moved, but no sound came out.

"Felix?"

My eyes snapped open. The room was dim, but I could just make out familiar lavender curtains. Knitted ornaments hung from the walls in delicate pastel patterns. I took a deep breath, inhaling the fresh floral incense.

"Felix, are you alright? I heard you cry out."

I turned to see Brie standing at the foot of the stairs. She was huddled in an absurdly fluffy blanket and held her lantern up high in front of her. Her long black hair was neatly hidden beneath a blue bonnet and dancing lambs once again lined the bottom of her nightgown.

Relief flooded through me. *I'm out. That's right. I'd been freed from Myva's curse for over a year now.* The false goddess was dead, and I was at my mate's home. I rubbed at my tired eyes and tried to slow my erratic breathing. "It was just a bad dream. I'm sorry for waking you."

"Well, at least you're up now." She sounded a little breathless and rushed toward me. Her bare feet padded against the wood floor before she set the lantern down on the table and dove into the couch. She kicked my blankets up, then snuggled into my side, placing her own massive blanket on top. The soft silk of her bonnet brushed against my chin as she wrapped her arms around my torso. "OK, so you were right, but don't be a jerk about it."

As if I'd do anything to jeopardize her keeping her hands on me. I wrapped an arm around her and buried my nose in her scent. Letting the comforting smell chase away the last remnants of my cursed prison. "What was I right about?" I asked.

"I heard a noise outside and I couldn't sleep," she confided, the words half mumbled into my chest.

"You live on a farm, sweetheart. You're going to be hearing noises for the rest of your life." My response earned a light swat. I bit back a laugh and held her tighter.

My normally reserved little lamb threw a leg around my own and pulled me closer. It wasn't hard to guess why. The poor thing was clearly still shaken up from before. "You'll be alright. I have you," I whispered, tracing small circles on her shoulder.

"Will you stay up with me?" she asked. "Just until daylight. Those things don't like the sun, right?"

"Of course I will." My hand slid into hers, taking the opportunity to lace our fingers together. "They'll burn right up if exposed to the sun. Morning will be here soon, too. You've got nothing to worry about."

She squeezed my hand tight and nodded. "What were you dreaming about?"

"Nothing."

"It's fine. You don't have to tell me," she sighed.

"No," I began. "I meant I dreamt of nothing. It's what I experienced when I was under Myva's curse. It's a little hard to explain, but it was like being trapped in a pit of darkness."

She didn't answer for a moment, then gave my hand another squeeze. "I'm sorry. That sounds really scary."

"It was," I admitted. "But it's over now."

Brie's shoulders tensed beneath my fingers. "And now I've got you trapped in another curse."

"It's fine." I slid my hand down the curves of her body, then grabbed her ass. "This one comes with benefits."

The sound of her giggles rang through the early morning air. *Shit. It's morning.* Telltale red and orange hues peeked through the hillside just beyond Brie's farm. It was still too early to notice the sun's rise unless she looked directly out the window, but I only had a few minutes tops before that damnable light illuminated the room. It was childish of me, but I pulled the blankets further over her head. Anything to make the moment last a little longer. When it ended, Brie would remember to be wary of me. She'll pull away and I'll be stuck waiting until the next time she lets her guard down. But for a moment, I was a little less scary than the noises outside. For a moment, she was mine.

Brie rubbed her cheek against my chest and held me tighter. "I'm going to be so pissed off if I'm not your fated mate."

My heart stopped. "What?"

She pulled the blanket further over her eyes, no doubt trying to hide her face from me. "I just...I really enjoy having you around. It seems weird and fast to develop feelings for you this early. But I did. Even though your wolf form scares the shit out of me sometimes, I don't think I want this to end."

"It won't," I said. A fierce surge of possessiveness hit deep in my bones. No one would take this from me. Not magic, not the sun, not even the absence of an imprint. Brie was my wife.

Her voice cracked as she spoke. "How do you know?"

I closed my eyes and reeled in the sudden urge to build a fortress around my lamb's home. "If we find out I haven't imprinted when the potion has worn off, I'll just drink it again."

Brie shifted against me, poking her head out from under the covers to look me in the eye. In a panic, I gazed out the window to see the sun had continued its infernal ascent into the sky. Without thinking, I moved her to lie on top of me and pulled the blankets over us. She yelped at the sudden movement, then steadied herself. "You're not drinking more of the love potion." Her voice was stern, as if reprimanding a petulant toddler.

"I'll drink an entire barrel of love potions if it means you stay with me." I grinned, took her hips, and ground her against my cock. "Just like this."

Her lips quirked, and she gave another light swat to my shoulder. "I'm being serious."

I held her tighter; the need to keep her close to me was almost overwhelming. "As am I. Lamb, if you think I'm letting you go after this, you must not have paid close attention to all those werewolf romances lining your shelves. We're a persistent lot."

She smiled down at me and cupped my face. I leaned into the soft touch, trying to commit the gesture to memory. "You deserve better than some faulty love potion," she whispered.

I didn't care. What I deserved was irrelevant. What I wanted was right here. Smiling down at me like she didn't have my world in her hands. "Tell me you'll stay," I demanded.

Her smile faltered, worry and indecision creeping into the big brown eyes I'd come to love so much. "Felix—"

"Don't," I said, stopping whatever excuse she was about to give. I gently gripped the back of her neck, running my thumb along the side. Her eyes fluttered closed, her lips parted with a sigh. "Lie to me if you have to. Just tell me you'll stay when this is over."

Her brow furrowed, and she bit her lip. I waited for her eyes to open again, barely breathing. When they did, the worry was still there, accompanied by unshed tears. "OK," she whispered, "I'll stay."

I pulled her down and kissed her hard. Letting the desperation and possessiveness I felt run free. I nipped at her lower lip and she let me in. Wasting no time in running her tongue along mine in a dance of needy promises. I took advantage of her submission and dragged her down further. Molding her body against mine until not an inch separated us. She didn't love me yet. I knew that, but dammit, she would.

When we broke for air, Brie lifted the covers off of us and I could no longer hide the sun from our little corner of the world. Her body relaxed when she looked out the window. "Hey, it's daylight," she breathed, a smile tugging at her swollen lips.

"Wonderful," I grumbled.

Brie's hands fidgeted against me, a timid expression on her face. "So, Fallon mentioned it would take him a few days to break through the jewel."

I nodded, unsure of where she was going.

"There's not much use in standing around worrying, so do you maybe want to...spend the day on a rowboat?" She glanced back at me. "I could show you around the safe parts of the bayou."

"Sweetheart," I said with all seriousness. Not bothering to hide the stupid grin on my face. "If I ever say no to that question, I want you to slap me."

Curse the rain and all that it stands for. Large droplets of date-ruining evil pounded against the roof. Mocking me. As soon as Brie and I had gotten dressed, the weather shifted in an instant. Clear blue skies darkened into angry clouds before a sea of bullshit rained down.

At my side, Brie let out a long sigh. "Well, that's too bad. Maybe it will clear up by the time I'm done with morning chores. The weather around here is unpredictable sometimes."

I'm not leaving it up to chance. "Lamb, I have an errand to run down by the docks. Are you going to be alright by yourself for an hour or so?" I asked.

"Sure." She patted my arm and headed out the door. "If you need me, I'll be knee-deep in sheep shearing."

I held up a hand to stop her before she stepped out into the rain. "Quick question. If you primarily use this farm for milk, why do you have sheep?" Most of Brie's livestock comprised a herd of pygmy goats, an angry-looking pinto stallion and three sheep thrown into the mix. It wasn't nearly enough wool to make a profit on.

She shrugged and pulled up the hood of her coat. "I just like to knit and they're cheap to keep."

Right. I should have guessed from all the knitted ornaments.

I nodded and waited for her to make her way to the barn. When she was safely out of sight, I shed my clothes and transformed. Shaking off the post-shift jitters, I took off into the rain and headed for the docks. Inclement weather wasn't about to get in my way. Not when there was a storm dragon around.

In my wolf form, it didn't take long to reach my destination. Angry-looking waves beat against our ship's hull. Yet the mighty *Banshee* hardly moved from her place in the docks. The large brig stood out against the smaller ships in Boohail's port. Villagers often wandered by trying to get a closer look inside. Most probably never having seen anything bigger than the quaint hulks used to ferry goods to neighboring towns. Though only a select few have been brave enough to ask the crew for a tour.

The last being a little girl by the name of Lottie. Whose mother damn near had a heart attack when she spotted her daughter riding around on the shoulders of an orc. It was a pity the humans were still terrified of us. But we did show up unannounced after killing their goddess. So, I suppose it would be even more strange if they weren't.

In my haste to board the ship, I almost ran straight into Holly. The centaur braced herself and moved her body to shield the woman behind her. "What's got you in such a huff?" she asked. "I figured you'd still be stalking your woman some-where."

"I am," I snapped. "No, wait. I mean, I am not stalking. Not anymore, anyway. She wants me around now."

Holly's brow raised, and she flipped her dark auburn hair over her shoulder.

"Right, sure."

"She does." Her disbelieving grunt had me digging my claws into the wood floor, but I had bigger fish to fry. "Have you seen Dante?"

A blond woman, Priscilla, if I remembered correctly, poked her head out from behind Holly. "I saw him head down to

Puffer Cove. It's just a short walk down the beach," she said, pointing to her left. Shortly after our merry band of misfits dispatched Myva, the former chosen hero and Holly became attached at the hip. I didn't think the sour-faced centaur would have much luck with the ladies. But I've been wrong before. Thankfully, they took pity on the rest of the single crew and kept their loud rendezvous to the human's home instead of the ship. Mostly.

Holly crossed her arms and shifted her weight to the side. An odd gesture to see on a half-horse frame. "What do you need with Dante?"

I wanted to rush past her, but Holly was a stubborn bull when it came to staying in people's business. "Brie and I are going on a date, and I need him to stop the rain."

Her stare was deafening. "Let me get this straight. You're going to ask a dragon, an actual titan creature, to stop the rain so you can go on a date."

Impatience twitched at the edge of my soaked tail. "What else does he have going on today? It's not like we're out robbing ships."

For a moment, the women just stared in silence. Holly shook her head. "I have to see this. Doll, hop on." She turned to help Priscilla on her back, then gestured in the direction of the cove. "Lead the way, dead man," she chuckled.

Ignoring her, I made my way down the beach. The sound of the bustling docks faded away against the rumbling thunder of the storm. A small trail was nestled in between massive rock formations. Once through, it led us to the cove and dragon in question. Dante had shed his human form, and was snoring peacefully amidst the thrashing waves beating against the coast. His long, serpent-like body was sprawled out amongst the jagged rocks surrounding the cove. Silver scales glittered against the pouring rain, giving the ancient creature an ethereal glow.

The clop of Holly's hooves came to a stop behind me. "Felix, do not wake him up," she said.

"I have to wake him up. I need the rain to stop."

Fear dripped onto the edge of her voice as she moved in front of me, blocking my path. "Forget the damn rain. Do not wake him up."

If I was a less desperate man, I might have heeded her warning. Under the normal rules of Volsog, you just didn't bother a titan-level creature. Well, unless you were suicidal. Krakens, giants, and dragons were in a league of their own. But this was Boohail, not Volsog. Dante wasn't some lord defending his territory, he was another crew member of the *Banshee*.

Even after Cinnamon and Fallon left the ship for their ridiculously long honeymoon, Dante stuck around and became part of our raiding party. Sailing the high seas and stealing from royal fleets was easy work when you had a creature who could control the weather. That and the fact that every ship we'd come across wanted nothing to do with a fight against a ship full of demons. As far as pirating went, it was rather boring. Why he continued to stick around, I wasn't sure. A dragon that old surely had a hoard somewhere he could draw on if he ever needed gold or money. If I was a betting man, I'd say the storm bringer just liked the company. Not that he'd ever admit that.

Priscilla furrowed her brow and looked between the dragon and me. "Why can't he wake him up?"

Holly sighed and pinched the bridge of her nose. "Dragons are proud, unpredictable creatures. You don't just go around asking them for favors and you sure as shit don't wake them up." She glared down at me and stomped her hoof. "Do you remember the damage that red dragon caused eight years ago? He scorched so much land we had to redraw the maps!"

"Just because someone woke him up?" Priscilla asked.

I tried taking a step around the centaur, but she blocked me. "We don't know why he did that," I growled. "For all we know, there could have been a perfectly good reason. Besides, Dante is one of us. He's not going to burn the world over a nap. Now move!"

"**I might**," came an impossibly deep voice. Holly tensed and turned around to see dark purple eyes glowing through the mist around the dragon's face. Dante stretched and yawned, showing rows of sword-length fangs. "**Let's hear it then. You must have a good reason for disturbing me.**"

Holly kept her eyes trained on the dragon and retreated behind the rocks.

"I do," I said, lifting my chin. "My wife and I are going on a date."

Thunder shook the ground beneath my feet before a strike of lightning hit a nearby tree. The tree snapped in half and fell uselessly into the sand. **"And you've come to rub your good fortune in my face?"**

Sensitive little bugger. "No. I need you to stop the rain. We can't go rowboating like this."

He rested his head along a boulder, his eyes drooped with the effort of staying conscious. **"What did you bring to trade?"**

"I'll give ya a heartfelt 'thanks,' friend."

He snorted. **"Try again."**

"Alright fine, what do you want?" I asked.

His lips quirked around jagged teeth. The familiar sinister glint in his eyes had my fur standing on ends. **"Let's just agree that you'll owe me a favor in the future."**

"Absolutely not," I barked out. Gods only knew what nefarious schemes he wanted to pull. "You owe me for that stunt you pulled with the barren rune, anyway. Just cut off this one storm for me and we'll call it even."

Behind me, Holly and her companion broke out into giggles. I guess it was easy to laugh at agonizing birth control when you never had to worry about pregnancy scares with your own partner.

"Nice try," Dante began. **"I did that at your request, out of the kindness of my heart."**

I bared my fangs at him. "You did it because you're a sadistic bastard. Pick something else."

He rolled his eyes. **"Fine. Three lemon meringue pies."**

"...Pies?" I asked. Of all the things I thought a dragon would ask for, sweets weren't one of them. "You eat pies?"

"No, I shove them up my ass," he growled. **"Yes, I eat them. There's a shop on Main Street called Sonia's Sweet Treats. I want three of her lemon meringue pies."**

"Oh, I love that place!" Priscilla spoke up. She clapped her hands together excitedly and smiled. "Sonia makes the best pies in Boohail. Holly, we need to go after this. Now I'm craving her chocolate peanut butter pies."

The dragon's head perked up. **"One of those, too. I wasn't able to try those before she banned me from the store."**

"OK, I'll bite," Holly sighed. "What did you do to get banned?"

His tail slammed into the ocean, sending a spray of water high into the air. **"I did nothing,"** he roared. **"She banned all horned creatures after fucking Warwick got his horns caught on a hanging lantern and crashed into her glass counter. Now I'm stuck pie-less because that stupid minotaur can't stop tripping over his own hooves. Usha said she'd pick up a few for me when she made her supply run, but I haven't seen her all day."**

Unsurprising. Warwick was as clumsy as a newborn fawn.

I couldn't even recall how many times we'd had to fish him out of the ocean after he fell overboard.

"And you're not just going to...take her pies?" Holly asked. Clearly thinking the same thing I was. There wasn't much one shop owner could do to stop someone as powerful as Dante from breaking into a bakery.

The dragon snorted, letting out a stream of flames. **"Who am I to tell her how to run her business?"**

"Alright, pies it is. So, can you stop the rain now?"

Dante nodded and stood. **"Just leave them in my quarters and the rain will be gone before you make it back to your wife."** His winding body uncoiled itself from the cove. With another clap of thunder, he shot up into the air. Dark, angry clouds parted in his wake as he wove himself into the sky.

"Well," Holly said, coming to my side. "That went way better than I thought it would."

Chapter 9

Brie

"That's not something you see every day."

Across from me, Felix glanced up but said nothing. I squinted and tried to focus on the massive dragon in the sky. It wasn't Fallon. His scales were pitch black. The dragon dove low beneath the clouds, then reared up again, showing off its silver coloring. In its wake, the angry clouds parted into shining sun and rainbows. When the beast wove back again, the light from the rainbows reflecting off his scales cast a ray of color on the trees below. "He must be that other dragon Fallon mentioned. Dillon or something."

Felix laughed, pausing his rowing to clutch at his sides.

"Is it not Dillon? I don't remember," I asked.

"No, please call him Dillon," he said, grinning.

After I had finished tending to my animals, the pouring rain had seemed to vanish as quickly as it had appeared. Stranger still, the storm vanished in irregular patches that didn't really make sense. After I left my barn, the clouds had all disappeared over my farm. But when I looked around, it was only my farm and a weird line in the sky coming from the direction of the beach. By the time I'd changed out of my soaked clothes, Felix had reappeared with a picnic basket and we set off toward the river for our date.

"What did you say your errand was again?" I asked.

"I didn't." He took hold of the paddles and resumed steering us down the river.

I waited for further explanation, but he merely smiled and remarked on a particularly colorful butterfly. "Alright, fine. I don't like learning secrets, anyway."

With fall in full swing, the leaves that made up the river's canopy were lit up in a blaze of color. Bulbous tupelo trees wound their way out of the water to champion their own foliage into the crowded sky. Moss draped over the branches, making up the meandering trail along the river bed, while the harsh midday sun was high in the air, which gave us a temporary reprieve from the bayou's army of mosquitoes. I'd lived here my whole life, yet I never got tired of how beautiful the land could be when the leaves turned.

We came to a fork in the river, and I directed Felix toward

the skinnier trail on the right. "If you want, we can go down that side another day. It leads through the village, and there are plenty of food stalls set up on shore this time of year. But there isn't much canopy and I don't feel like sweating."

Felix dug an oar into the water and let it turn the boat down the proper path. With one more firm push, the smaller river's current caught the boat, and he relaxed back in his seat. "Excellent, I'm still getting used to how unbearably hot it gets here." He fanned out his loose white shirt to emphasize his point.

Stop staring at his collarbone, you little pervert.

"Did it not get very hot in Volsog?" I asked, taking a sharp interest in anything that wasn't Felix's broad chest.

"It gets a little warm after the dark season, but nothing like this." He brushed back his blond hair and fetched a bottle of mead and a few glasses out of the basket. He mentioned that he'd dropped by Cinnamon's on the way back and I was more than a little excited to see what that foodie packed for us.

"What's a dark season?" I took my drink and helped him set up the boat's middle bench for the array of food he'd brought with him. Soon the bench was lined with sandwiches, cracklins, boudin balls, an assortment of fruits, a small blueberry pie, and various other treats. My mouth watered when I caught sight of Cinnamon's signature meat pies. If she'd made those with me in mind, then I was in for a fiery treat.

Felix raised a brow at me. "You know, the dark season." At

my confused look, he continued. "When the sun goes away for the second half of the year."

"Are…are you messing with me?" I asked.

His eyes widened, and he looked at the sky as if the sun would give him answers. "Do you not have a dark season here? The snow must get miserably high if it stays warm enough all winter."

I clutched my drink to my chest and piled food on my plate. "Felix, I've never even seen snow before."

His mouth dropped open. "It just stays warm here? Is that why you have so little food stored in your pantry? I thought the village had been hit with a terrible famine and you lost your winter supplies."

"You've gotta stop rummaging through my things."

Felix cleared his throat and looked away. "It's my duty to ensure that you wouldn't starve in the cold months. I only wanted to see how much hunting I'd have to do."

"How gallant," I replied dryly.

He nodded, pleased. "I'm glad you understand."

I shook my head and took a sip of my drink. "Boohail's been hit with a lot of things, but a food shortage has never been one of them. Even when it floods, there's still plenty of fish to go around. What kind of hell-scape have y'all been living in?"

I couldn't even imagine not seeing the sun for a few days, let alone several months. When the demons' pirate ship landed on our shores, I assumed they stuck around because Cin and

Fallon were here. But maybe they just didn't want to go back to whatever frozen wasteland they came from.

He looked down at the food spread out on the bench and shook his head.

"A starving one, apparently. You'd never find this wide variety of food back there. To be honest, I don't even know what half of this stuff is. Cinnamon just packed the basket and sent me out the door when I asked her for help." He pointed to a cup of mango slices and shrugged.

"Oh, you poor baby. Not even the mangoes?"

"Especially not the mangoes. Fruit was rare, and normally too expensive to bother with." He took a hesitant bite, then nodded in approval. "Damn that's sweet." He polished off another slice. "Wars would have been fought over this."

I giggled and took a bite of the meat pie. "A war over mangoes? You can't be serious."

His expression turned grave. "Darling, I'm about to go to war over them now." He popped a cracklin into his mouth and paused. "These crunchy things, too. If we rally all the demons in the area, we can take the south side of Kinnamo within the year and divert all agriculture into mangoes and crunchy things."

Laughter nearly made me choke on my food, and I covered my mouth to avoid spitting pie everywhere. "If that's your reaction to cracklins, I can't wait to see you try a boudin ball." When he looked around, unsure, I pointed out the meaty treat.

He took one and made a show of inspecting it before taking a bite. His eyes closed, a long sigh escaping as he took in the flavors. I reeled in my giggling to take a sip of mead while I waited for his approval. "Well?" I asked.

Felix glared off into the distance. "I'm shaken, I'm dismayed, I'm plotting battle strategies. The south side may not be enough. If this keeps up, we'll just have to rule all of Kinnamo with an iron fist."

"Cin's cooking will do that to ya," I said. My companion reached for a meat pie and I stopped him. "Hold on, are you alright with spicy food? Cin knows I like this extra hot, so that may be too much for you."

Felix's mouth quirked, and he gave me a challenging look. "So long as it's not cheese filled, I'm sure I'll be fine."

"Hun, I promise this isn't a shot at your manhood. You don't need to prove me wrong. That pie will burn your mouth if you're not used to it."

"Well, now I feel like I've been issued a challenge."

Before I could stop him, he snatched a meat pie and took a large bite.

I sighed and sat back in my chair to watch the show. Felix grinned triumphantly and kept chewing. Two seconds ticked by. Panic crept into his eyes, but he kept chewing, trying to save face. "Feeling the burn yet?" I asked.

He shook his head and placed his hands on his knees. Then leaned back again to thrum his fingers against the bench.

Soon his eyes began to water, his face turned redder than a cayenne, and he could no longer contain his coughing fit. I took pity and handed him a flask of water. "Did she imbue it with the souls of the damned?" he sputtered around the flask. "I've been burned with fire less hot than this."

"I tried to warn you," I said, finishing off my pie.

He coughed into his elbow. "You made it look so easy."

I shrugged. "What can I say? I'm sustained by the souls of the damned."

His voice took on a concerned edge as I munched on my second pie. "Your ass is going to regret that later."

"Eh, it can take a tentacle, it can take a pie." I winced when I realized what had come out of my mouth. My dirty jokes had earned the ire of my last two lovers and so I tried to avoid them on the first date. I could still see the disapproving hard line in Victor's jaw. Nice body, but man, the guy could be a wet blanket. Instead of a disgusted sneer, Felix laughed so hard the boat shook. I steadied my glass and trapped the bottle of mead between my legs so it didn't tip over.

"Well, at least our sense of humor matches," I said, smiling.

His laughter died down and he refilled our glasses. "I should hope we match. We're married after all."

I couldn't stop my eyes rolling if I wanted to. "Threatening some poor clerk into doing what you want is hardly a decla-ration of a love match."

"Is that all I have to do to win you?" he asked. Felix's eyes darkened and my heart skipped a beat. He kept his gaze fixed on mine and set down his glass. "If I shout how much I want you from the rooftops, will you fall into my arms?"

Did it suddenly get hotter?

I swallowed and tried to tuck my hair behind my ear until I remembered that I put it up in a bun. "I...don't think you have to go that far."

"How far should I go then?" he whispered.

I jumped when our boat hit the bank of a small clearing. The heat from Felix's gaze left me a little breathless. "Oh look, these wildflowers are still in full bloom. Maybe we should finish our lunch here." Without waiting for an answer, I stood and gathered up the remaining foods back into the basket.

He turned toward the clearing and gave a half smile. "Wildflowers, eh? The gods must be smiling on us."

Felix hopped off the boat and held his hand out to me. My stomach fluttered when I took it. He paused to fish out a blanket from beneath his seat and tossed it over his shoulder. We made our way further into the meadow as I tried to stomp down my nervousness. You'd think at twenty-six a woman would learn how to not act like a love-struck teen. Yet the longer he held my hand, the more dangerous the threat of sweaty palms became.

Finally, he released my hand and spread the blanket out for us. I let out a breath of relief and set the basket down.

Before I could turn to sit, Felix grabbed my wrist and pulled me down on top of him. My long skirt hitched up around my thighs and I yelped as he settled me on his lap. The scent of sandalwood and man put me in a choke hold. "Are you going to answer my question?" he asked, moving a hand to grab the back of my neck.

This close, I could see the tiniest splash of green just below his pupils. A dark ring of sapphire encased the icy blue that made up the rest of his iris. The barest hint of freckles sprinkled along his cheeks. So faint I'd never noticed it before. Felix was stunning, and it only made the nervous fireflies in my gut flutter faster. "It doesn't count as falling if you pull me into your arms."

Felix grinned, the small dimple on his left cheek making its grand appearance. "No, I suppose it doesn't. Forgive me, Lamb. Every day, it's more difficult to keep my hands off you." His free hand rested on my hip. I shuddered as I felt his fingers dip just below my blouse to run along the exposed skin. "It'd be nice to be able to take things slow and do normal couple things. Visit your house on a rainy day and forget some trinket, so I have an excuse to come back for it. Make the most out of the little times we spend together."

My eyes fluttered closed as he ran his lips along my throat. I swallowed and clenched at his shirt, my fingers digging into the soft fabric.

The heat of his breath against my neck felt more potent than any aphrodisiac.

"Yet, in the same breath, I resent any interference that

takes me away from you. Even for a brief moment." His wandering lips grew bolder and traced along my collarbone before he slipped my blouse down off my shoulders. My breath came out in ragged pants when his other hand slipped completely under my shirt to trace along my back.

"I want to hang my coat next to your door and place my boots at your entryway, so anyone who comes to see you knows that there's a man in your life. I want to place my clothes in your dresser so our scents mix together." His voice lowered to a hungry growl against my breast. "I want a great many things and I honestly just don't know how to be patient about it."

This man could picture a life with me so clearly, and I could barely make up my mind about breakfast. Whether I wanted him back wasn't a question anymore. I did. I really did. Yet my relationships had never gone past casual dating before and I didn't even know what love was supposed to feel like. Being near him felt right. Maybe that was it.

Before I could withdraw into my sea of self-doubt, I took his face in my hand and kissed him. All at once, a bright spark lit up in my body, releasing something akin to fire in my blood. Hungry and all-consuming. I pulled away, a little disoriented from the intensity of the feeling.

His eyes looked hazy and unfocused. "Brie?"

All I could focus on was his nearness. My heart beat against my rib cage as if it were the one suffering the effects of the potion. "I think I might love you," I whispered.

His cheeks flushed, his eyes widened and suddenly I was in the air. The sound of ripping fabric and my yelp filled the meadow. I landed with a hard thud against a fur covered chest, my skirt nearly flipping over my head. I battled the fabric back down to decency, then paused when realization dawned. Felix had transformed. Cold fear crept down my spine as I took in the werewolf that was sprawled on his back underneath me.

Quickly, he sat upright, knocking me back on my bum. Clawed hands reached out to grab me, but he shrank back when I flinched.

"I'm sorry—" Felix cut himself off as his hands fidgeted, his long tail beating the surrounding flowers into an early grave. "I mean, I didn't mean to change."

I sat upright and rubbed at my lower back. *That's gonna sting in the morning.*

Still a fidgeting mess, Felix gathered up his tattered clothes, shoved them in front of his crotch, and turned away from me. Then slammed a hand down on his overzealous tail. "Just give me a minute," he called back.

Well, that might just be the cutest thing I've ever seen. The massive werewolf form still set me on edge. But it was hard to be terrified of him when he was so beside himself.

Felix glanced back at me before snapping his head forward. His ears fell flat on his head. "This is so embarrassing," he muttered to himself.

I laughed and came to sit beside him. "This isn't going to

happen during sex, right? I'm open to a lot of things, but this feels like a hard limit."

He buried his face in his hands. "It never has before."

"I'll take your word for it."

He kept his eyes closed and slowed his breathing. Soon, the hackles on the back of his neck lowered. After a few more breaths, I was once again looking at the much less hairy version of Felix. He inspected his hands, then nodded when their lack of claws was confirmed.

A pink flush remained firm across his face. "Is there... any way we could try that again?" he asked.

I cocked my head. "Did you want me to tell you I love you again or were you just aiming to throw me in the river?" I put a fist to my chin and hummed. "I didn't peg you for the vengeful type, but I suppose I've thrown quite a few things at you already."

A grin tugged at the corner of his mouth. "Keep up the attitude and I just might."

"You wouldn't dare."

Felix's eyes took on a predatory glint, and I leapt up to race away from him. Cursing my choice in attire, I hiked up my long skirt until the purple fabric smacked again over the tops of snapdragons. Behind me, the werewolf lunged forward, and I shrieked, barely dodging his attempt.

My stubby legs put forth a good fight, but they were no match in the end. Strong arms enclosed around my waist, and

Felix hoisted me up over his shoulder. Wild giggles bubbled out of my throat as I steadied my hands on his back. However, my laughter was cut short when I noticed Felix was actually carrying me towards the river. "Wait, no!"

He slapped my ass and kept going. "It's too late for pleading, darling. Vengeance is mine."

I beat against his back and tried to wiggle free. "Felix I -Don't-Know-Your-Middle-Name Monet, if you get my hair wet, then this marriage is over!"

The cool water of the river splashed around his ankles as he took his first steps in. "You know what I want, Lamb."

"Oh, you horrible extortionist," I growled. He tightened his grip when I thrashed harder. When he moved to hold me in front of him, I caved. "Alright, fine," I yelped, clutching his shoulders.

He hooked an arm under my butt and waited. "Well?"

"I'm sorry," I muttered.

"What else?"

"Don't be greedy."

Felix hummed. "Alright, enjoy your life as a water nymph." His grip loosened.

I cried out and wrapped my arms around his chest. "Fine! I sort of maybe love you a little bit." Heat rose in my face when the words finally came out.

"I'm sorry, sweetheart, I wasn't listening. One more time?" he said, tightening his hold.

I scrunched my nose and looked away. "I said I might love you a little bit. Alright? Don't get a big head about it."

His body shuddered. Soft lips met my own in a fevered kiss. Felix gripped my ass and hauled me up against him so I could wrap my legs around his torso. I slid my arms around his shoulders, gasping for breath as he kissed my throat. His long legs made quick work of returning us to the blanket before he sat down with me straddling his lap. His insistent hands tore at my top, sending wild tremors of lust through my body. The fire in my veins held more desperation than I ever knew I was capable of feeling.

And Felix, Felix touched me in a way that was akin to reverence. When he tore off my top, I expected him to go straight to my breasts, as most men did. To the credit of men long past, I have an impressive rack. One perk of being a woman of weight is that you often had the chest to match all those late-night cheese plates. Yet instead, his hands glided down the expanse of my shoulders, his tongue mapped the slope of my neck before exploring my collar bone. I shuddered, my fists grabbing handfuls of his hair as he continued his slow, deliberate survey.

He drank me in like fine wine. Pausing from my collar to taste the mead on my lips. The kiss broke as he hooked his thumbs under my breast band and pulled it over my head, tossing it away. The shimmering blue in his eyes let loose the sea of emotion hiding underneath. This man fucking loved me. If the obvious devotion and admiration in his gaze wasn't enough, he showed it in the careful way he laid me down. In the gentle caresses he ran along my body. In the way he stopped running his hands along my hip when I flinched from my damn ticklishness, only to move on to running his tongue along my nipple until I moaned underneath him. I'd never been touched like this. Like some precious treasure worth guarding. Felix loved me and I couldn't tell if it was terrifying or exhilarating.

This could end so badly. In no less than a week, this man had me wrapped around his finger. If the heartbreak ending came to pass, then I was going to be a wreck missing this kind of all-consuming affection.

His rough hands slid my skirts down past my ankles before pulling them free. I watched on, entranced, as he kissed the side of my ankle, running his hands down the smooth skin of my leg. As if no part of me was worth rushing through. Heat surged to my core with every kiss he trailed down my leg.

A deep, insecure voice in my head said I didn't deserve this. That there was no way something like becoming a fated mate to a beautiful, fun werewolf would ever happen to me of all people. Maybe it was right. Or maybe it could go fuck itself. For now at least, there was nothing stopping me from getting lost in the heady feeling of being wanted. The inescapable blaze of lust that followed his touches.

Suddenly, his gentle explorations weren't enough. My body ached and my pussy clenched around nothing, as it voiced its displeasure at still being empty. *You and me both, sis.*

I gasped when he ran a thumb down the slick folds of my pussy.

Felix groaned, letting his thumb tease circles around my clit. "You're so wet for me already, Lamb." Gods, he had a voice that bathed you in sunshine after a cold rain. The desperation in my core threatened to explode if I didn't feel his cock sink into me.

I took Felix by the chin, guiding him back to me for a kiss. The taut muscles of his frame grew hot under my touch and I flipped him over so I could straddle him. His eyes flared. The thick head of his cock pulsed against my inner thigh. I bit my lip and dragged my pussy across its hot length. I considered slowing down to explore every dip in his ridiculously cut abs for a while, but I was greedy, and my body insisted on the main event. If I had my way, there would be plenty of time afterwards to investigate each and every minute detail.

Giving in, I reached between us to line up the head of his cock against my folds. He let out a gasp, and I paused, raising an eyebrow at him. "I need you to tell me you're not going to transform again if I keep touching you."

Felix ran his hands up my thighs. Teasing them further apart so he could get a better look. "Sweetheart, if it means I get to watch you sink down on my cock, I will swear on my life to never shift again."

I laughed and let the head of his dick sink just inside me before rising again. Teasing his sensitive flesh. "I don't need you to go that far."

His hands locked on my hips, but he made no move to push me down further onto him. I sank a little deeper, letting out a moan when the tight muscles around my entrance flexed around him. "Yes," he hissed. "Work yourself on my cock. Show me you can take it."

With every inch I gave him, Felix kept his hooded eyes trained on where our bodies joined. His breath came out in ragged pants until his head fell back with a groan when I finally sank to the hilt.

My body shivered with sensation, and I rose again, before slamming myself back down. I cried out, unable to even bother trying not to. Not with the perfect way his dick curved upward. Hitting that deep, glorious spot that had me seeing stars.

His grip tightened and the next time I thrust down, he ground me down against him. Highlighting the delicious friction until all thoughts of teasing him flew out the window. I braced myself on his shoulders and began bouncing on his cock in earnest.

"Atta girl," he whispered. I choked out a sob when he dipped his hand to my pussy, letting the thrust of our hips brush my clit against his fingers. "You're such a good fucking girl, aren't you?" The aroma of wildflowers mixed with Felix's intoxicating scent. My senses grew weak against the onslaught of pleasure. "You can ride me faster than that, can't you? Of course you can."

Moaning out some jumbled nonsense, I tried to work myself

faster to give in to his demand. My body coiled tighter. So wet I could hear the slippery sounds every time I thrust back onto him. "Oh, gods."

"They're not going to help you now, Lamb." A hint of red flashed in his eyes before it faded back to blue. Felix moved a hand to grip the back of my neck while the one on my hip helped slam me down.

"Felix?" I slowed my pace and looked him over. He blinked and then met my gaze with a grin. No trace of the red in his eyes remained.

He sat up and rolled us until I was flat on my back. I shuddered when he pulled out just before the tip and thrust back in. His movements were slow and sure. Sinking into my tight channel with enough command to ensure I felt every inch of him. My inner walls clenched around him. Never in my life had I felt so stretched and full and—gods help me—desperate for more.

He shifted his weight, threw one of my legs over his shoulder, and when he moved again, I broke. Throwing my head back in a strangled cry, lightning dancing across my skin at the force of the surprise orgasm. He groaned low in his throat. Progressively increasing his speed to the point where I was screaming his name and clawing at his back. Encouraging him to work me through my orgasm until the pleasure was so blinding I had half a mind to travel to Volsog, find whoever raised this man, and introduce the hell out of myself.

When did I lose control of the situation?

"Sorry, love. I just don't feel like sharing you right now." If I wasn't so drunk off my orgasm, I might have noticed sooner how loud his heart was beating. How his eyes flashed from the normal blue to a deadly looking red. "No one is going to take you from me," he declared in a voice so feral it was almost unhinged. Felix slid a hand between us and stroked my clit while still pumping in and out of me, capturing my lips in a possessive kiss.

His gentleness was gone. Replaced with a fierce greed and impatience akin to a starving man. I shivered as he tasted my throat. Running his lips along the sensitive skin until I felt the brush of sharp fangs against the juncture between my neck and shoulder. Felix growled and sped up his movements, just before sinking his teeth into my neck. Not enough to break the skin, but just enough to send a wild thrill of pain through me. In the blink of an eye, I was spiraling again. Like a helpless bird caught in the riptide of rushing rapids. As my walls clamped down on him again, Felix's body seized, and he roared his release. Before collapsing on top of me and sliding over to the side, he thrust a couple more times. The spasms of ecstasy made his body tremble.

After a few moments of panting and trying to form coherent thoughts, my soul finally floated back down to my body. I had assumed, with the lack of a tentacle monster, the next time we had sex wouldn't leave me such a panting mess. But dammit, sometimes it's good to be wrong.

At my side, Felix sat stone-still with his head resting on his knees. There was a low thumping noise emanating off the werewolf and his fingernails had extended to claws. *Oh shit.* "Um…did you need to go again?" My body was sore, but the last time his heart thumped like that, we wound up going all night. Maybe once wasn't enough to calm the curse down.

I sat up and looked around for my scattered clothes. "Are you well enough to make it back to my house first? As exciting as outdoor sex is, you're in for a wicked sunburn if we stay out here all day."

He closed his eyes and took a deep breath. "Lamb, please tell me I didn't break the skin on your neck."

"Oh, you mean the bite?" I rubbed my hand along the mark he left, and it came back clean. "No, there's no blood."

"Good. I'm sorry for losing control like that," he said, his body slumping in relief.

Our shoulders brushed as I moved closer to him and gave his arm a comforting squeeze. "We got a little rough. It's no big deal."

Felix lifted his head, and I froze when blood-red eyes peered at me. "I'm not apologizing for rough sex, Lamb. I'm sorry, because I almost turned you into a werewolf."

Chapter 10

Brie

"You...what?" My body felt numb as I grabbed the mark on my neck. His body thrummed with the frantic beat of his heart. Felix took my hand away and turned to kiss the angry bruise forming.

"It was terrible and reckless of me. But you smell so good. Every time you so much as look at me, I want to claim you."

I fell back under his weight, his hand trapping my wrist to the ground. "Is that not what we've been doing?" I asked. Heat pooled in my lower belly as Felix kissed his way down my chest, flicking his tongue against my nipple.

"No, sweetheart," he chuckled. He pushed my legs apart and kissed my mouth so deeply, the world spun. The thick head of his cock rocked against my opening.

Oh, fuck yes.

With a low grunt, Felix thrust to the hilt inside me. I gasped at the rough intrusion. My body shivered with a delicious ache it knew he could satisfy. "This is all I can do to ease my obsession for you. What I want is to turn you. Brand my mark into your flesh until you feel the same need I do. I want every demon to take one whiff of you and know this cunt belongs to me."

Sweet dancing baby goats. This man is a monster made out of every book lover I've ever pined over. My body sang with sensation, chasing away my weariness into a distant memory. "Let's get this love potion off you before we start changing my species, alright?"

His body stilled, and he searched my face as if he were seeing it for the first time. "Are you saying you're not opposed to me turning you?"

I ran a hand through his blond curls, brushing the soft tresses out of his face. "I can't say I've put much thought into the idea. Am I going to develop your allergy to cheese?"

His eyes widened, and he shook his head. "No. You'll be a turned werewolf. You won't be as strong as a full-blooded one like me, but you shouldn't suffer any adverse effects." Felix spoke in hushed tones. The harsh thump of his heartbeat against my chest.

"So I gain extra strength and better senses. I'm not going to turn into a howling twat during the full moon, am I?"

He grit his teeth. "The first shift maybe. After that, the urge fades."

That didn't seem like too bad of a deal in the scheme of things. It was clear as day that turning me meant something to him. Not that I was surprised. In every werewolf romance I've read, if the heroine is a human at the start, she normally ends up getting turned at the end. I wasn't ready to give up my human card just yet. But the idea wasn't a terrible one.

"Ask me again when our two weeks are up. I might say yes."

The cock still firmly planted inside of me twitched. The thick base began to swell, and I shivered in anticipation. "You might say yes," he breathed.

I nodded and ran my hands down his back. "If it's confirmed that I am your fated mate, then you can turn me." I held up a finger in warning. "But not a second sooner."

His face broke out into a grin before he rocked into me. My legs came around his waist to hold him closer. I closed my eyes to savor how good his skin felt on mine. Yet a noise in the distance caught my attention. I looked toward it, scanning the river for any signs of an intruder.

Felix held my chin and forced me to look at him. "Eyes on me, gorgeous."

Lord have mercy.

In the distance, a soft feminine voice rang out. Growing closer. "On our left you'll find a pink one-legged bird, also known as the flappy flap. Some say flappy flaps can unhinge their jaw and swallow a man whole. It's me. I say that."

I swatted Felix's hand off my chin to see where the voice was coming from. "Do you not hear that?"

The man only groaned and thrust harder. "If there's someone there, then let them watch. I'm not done with you."

Ignoring him, I sat up on my elbows to get a better look around. But the only moving things I could see were a flamingo and a log floating down the river. It had something long and metal sticking out of it, but from what I could tell, no one was around.

"Oh, now this is a real treat, Barbara! On our right, you'll see the shapely ass of some muscular heartthrob as he absolutely goes to town on the woman beneath him. Just look at that form. It's a wonder and a marvel that her intestines haven't been crushed into oblivion, what with that massive horse cock Blondy's slinging," said the disembodied voice.

Heat raced across my face, and I shoved Felix off me. "Yeah no, the mood is over, get off."

He sighed in defeat and rolled onto his back, throwing an arm over his eyes. "Alright you little pervert, show yourself," he said, loud enough for his voice to carry over the meadow.

The voice took on a mocking tone. "Crikey Barbara, I think we've angered the yellow fella! That's just the kind of risks we have to take on these nature excursions."

Snatching my breast band off the ground, I quickly covered myself and tried again to find the voice. "Where are you?" I snapped.

174

"Where are any of us?" the voice called. "Do we even have free will, or are we just hunks of carbon floating in the endless abyss? Merely stuck in the back of an alligator hoping one day the slow fucker meanders to the ocean?"

"That was oddly specific," I said.

Felix rose from his spot next to me and made his way to the river. The voice whooped and hollered about the majesty of his abs, then fell silent as he shifted and dove into the water.

The log immediately changed course and darted towards Felix. A low hissing sound came out of the water before a ridged back appeared just above the surface. *Oh shit, she literally meant an alligator.*

I rushed to the water's edge and tried to wave off my were-wolf. "Felix, get out of the water! It's a gat—"

Angry hissing cut off with a crack. The two bodies thrashed violently, sending enormous splashes into the air. I watched through trembling fingers and hoped Felix was just as handy at fighting gators as he was ghouls. After what seemed like days, a mass of blond fur emerged from the water. Felix stood, carrying the gator in one hand and a sword in the other. He threw the massive reptile onto the bank and stuck the sword into the dirt. The werewolf held up a hand when I tried to approach him, then backed away from me to shake off the water.

"Well, I don't know about you, but I am seduced," said the voice.

I looked at the sword in the sand. "Did... did you say that?"

"I did," a chipper voice came. "Name's Alexis, nice to meet ya. I'd shake your hand, but alas, I am but a sword."

My deeply polite upbringing compelled a matching greeting. "Nice to meet you too, I'm Brie. Follow up question..." I gestured wildly at the sword and dead gator. "...How?"

Felix emerged at my side. He had switched back into his human form and had wrapped his tattered shirt around his waist like a loincloth. It was then I realized that I was still mostly naked. He wrung more water out of his hair and slung an arm around my shoulder. "Let me guess, you're the result of a fox demon's curse, right?" he asked.

Sun glimmered off worn metal. "That is a fantastic guess," the sword said, bemused. "Do you know my creator, Lucca? White hair, dark skin, wine snob?"

My werewolf's normally cheerful demeanor had soured. Instead of his damn near-permanent grin, he glared down at the sword as if it were the cause of all his struggles. It was a little unnerving. So I nudged his ribs playfully. "Lucca's not some jealous ex I have to worry about, are they?"

His mouth formed a thin line, and the arm around my shoulders grew stiff.

In front of us, the sword gasped. "Oh, burning silver plates, he is! You do know my creator!"

Felix grimaced and dropped his hand to the small of my back. "I swear you have nothing to worry about, Lamb. It was just a fling that ended years ago. I could just smell his magic on the sword. He pulled the same prank on Yala after the two got into a spat." The hand on my back twitched, reminding me of his frantic tail anytime he was in werewolf form.

"Tell me everything!" the sword shouted.

Felix scowled at the weapon before turning back to me. I held up a hand to stop his panic. "It's fine," I began. "I was just making a joke. You had a life before we met, so did I."

Slowly, his posture relaxed as he searched my face. He let out a breath and the worried crease in his brow vanished. If I was being honest, the knowledge of a past lover came with a bit of relief. If Felix was a blushing virgin, then I could only imagine how awkward our encounters would have been. Not that I had guessed he was a virgin after spending a night with him. There's no way someone was that good at sex just off the bat. Maybe if our relationship didn't pan out, I could work out joint custody of his tongue.

"Well, that was anticlimactic," Alexis grumbled.

"Where is your master?" Felix asked. "If you're here, he shouldn't be too far."

"That's where you're wrong, pretty boy! I've traveled all the way here from Goldcrest City. No Lucca in sight. I'm an independent woman, after all."

"How?" I asked. "Alligators don't live that far north."

Goldcrest was at least a full week away on horseback. I had no idea what that translated to in gator miles, though it couldn't have been any faster.

The sword's voice took on a smug tone. "My own ingenuity."

When neither Felix nor I responded, she huffed. "Fine. I got stolen while Lucca and his mate were visiting a bathhouse. I kept my mouth shut because the bandit who took me mentioned heading towards a port and I want to see the ocean. But his stupid ass got attacked by Barbara and I've been stuck in her back ever since."

"Where's the bandit?"

"In Barbara," she replied.

"Oh." I didn't really know what else to say to that.

"Don't pity him, he sucked. Even tried to sell some poor girl to that creepy claw cult a few towns over. And he never even bothered to oil me properly. Can you believe that? I can practically feel myself rusting away!"

"Wait, go back. What's this about a claw cult?" I asked.

I got the distinct feeling the sword just rolled her eyes. If she had any. "You know, those weirdos in red cloaks. They approached Fisher. That's the unlucky son of a bitch in Barbara, by the way, and asked him to bring women to their cult compound or whatever."

Felix and I shared a look. "Do you know where their compound is located?" Felix asked. "A few women in Boohail have gone missing."

"I do!" she chirped.

We waited for her to continue. But the sword fell silent. "Are you going to tell us?" I urged.

"Take me to the beach and I will."

I growled in frustration. "Are you serious right now? If you know where those missing girls might be, then fess up."

"I'll fess up on a beach surrounded by man booty. Preferably mermen, if ya got 'em."

"You little shit. We don't have time to throw you a damn beach party." The audacity of this hunk of junk was going to give me gray hair.

Felix put a hand on my shoulder and squeezed. "Stay calm, Lamb. There's an easier way of making her talk." His eyes darkened in a way that sent chills down my spine. "Get dressed," he said, patting my shoulder. "I know just the man to send our new friend to."

The sword let off an excited gasp. "Is it a merman?"

Fallon, leaning back against an oak tree, glared down at the sword. Even though I'd seen him the day prior, the dragon shifter looked as if he hadn't slept in weeks.

Dark bags had formed under his eyes and his normally shining black hair had dulled. "I'm going to ask you one more time. Where is this cult located?"

Alexis didn't answer. Once we arrived back at Cinnamon's home, the sword had loudly declared her demands and fell silent. Unfortunately, Fallon hadn't been able to undo the protection wards around the crystal yet. The most he had been able to identify in the past day was that it was made by a group of mages instead of just one. With six different magical signatures swirling around one object, it was going to be more than a few days' work trying to untangle their web. Which meant our greatest hope of finding my friend and the others was a crazy sword demanding a beach party.

The dragon shifter closed his eyes and took a deep breath. "Rabbit," he called. "Does this tree hold any value to you?" he said, motioning to the tree he was leaning on.

Cin raised a brow at him, then shook her head. "No."

"Good." Fallon pushed himself off the tree and grabbed the sword. He took one look at the silent hunk of metal, then immediately began slashing at the hard oak.

Tree bark sprayed around him from the violent force of his swing. Alexis screamed and cursed at him anytime her blade met wood. "Stop!" she wailed. "This is not my intended purpose! I cut flesh and emotions. This bark will dull my blade!"

Fallon took another slash at the tree, then stopped. "Are you going to tell us what you know?"

"My demands are reasonable," she sobbed. "I just want to go to the beach and see half-naked men running around. The way nature intended."

"Hmm...not the answer I'm looking for." He lifted her up and walked toward the road.

"Where are you taking me?" Alexis asked.

"You're looking a little dull. So I'm finding something to polish you with."

"For real? That'd actually be really nice. It's been a while since—" She paused as Fallon stopped near something on the ground. "THAT IS DEER SHIT!"

The demon's face twisted in what I can only describe as an evil grin and he lowered the tip of her blade toward the pile of poop.

"You better do what he says," Felix warned her. "He gets a little crazy without his beauty sleep. He'll do it."

"It won't stop here either," Fallon said, with a sinister gleam in his eye. "Brie has an entire farm full of goats and sheep. Maybe we'll use you to scrap out her stalls. How does that sound?"

It sounds like it will ruin my floors. But it's for the cause, I guess.

Just before steel met poop, Alexis caved. "OK, I'll talk! Just please don't put me in deer shit!"

"Well?" Fallon asked, lifting her away from the shit.

An aggravated yowl came off from the sword. "Doncaster! Those creepy cultists paid my bandit to bring women to an old fort on the outskirts of Doncaster. We didn't go in, but that's where the men told him to drop off any women he captured. Though he got eaten before he could grab anyone."

"Good riddance to him," Cin huffed.

"Doncaster," Fallon repeated. "How far away is that?"

"It's about a three-day journey on horseback," Cin said. "If you rest tonight, then you should be able to fly there in a few hours. Though if we're still aiming to sneak up on them, then we should probably land in the surrounding forests at night."

"That will have to do," Fallon sighed. "With any luck, we'll get there before the stolen women arrive and intercept them. For now, let's inform Usha and her men of the situation. Between Dante and me, we should be able to carry the full crew. With how advanced this magic is, I'm not taking any chances."

Cin crossed her arms and narrowed her eyes at him. "I'm going."

Her husband regarded her with a look of pure exasperation. "What happened to the terrified human that was too scared to leave her farm?"

"She fucked a dragon and helped kill a god." Cinnamon shrugged. "It changes a gal."

Fallon paused. As did the rest of us. It was hard to argue with that kind of logic. Whatever had happened in the year that Cin was gone had changed her. She stood taller, spoke more confidently, and from the looks of it, was no longer terrified of the bayou. She looked like she did before we lost Cherry. Her new husband and friends were unnerving to say the least, but if they're the ones that were able to heal Cin's heart, then they were good in my book.

"I like her," Alexis whispered.

"Me too," Fallon replied.

Felix came to my side and put a hand on my shoulder. "Lamb, I'm going to the ship to help them prepare for tomorrow. I'll be back well before nightfall. Think you can stay with Cin and Fallon until then?"

"Are there daytime ghouls?" I asked.

"Not to my knowledge."

"Then yeah, sure, I'll see you at home."

He kissed my forehead. My heart did a stupid little skip, and then Felix shifted and ran off. I turned to see Cin grinning ridiculously. "Shut up," I muttered.

She let out a giggle and covered her mouth. "I take it your little date went well?"

"It was fine," I said, thanking the gods for having dark enough skin to hide a blush.

"She's being coy!" Alexis shouted. "He had her bent six ways till Sunday in a meadow."

I clenched my fists and tried to remember a time before talking swords and bullshit.

Fallon handed the talking antagonizer back to me and slumped off back inside the house. "Trying to break that ward magic really did a number on him, huh?" I asked Cin.

"He'll be alright in the morning," she said. "Fallon is still young by dragon standards, so using his magic is extremely taxing."

"How old is he?"

Cin put a fist to her chin and gazed off. "I think he just turned one hundred and twenty-five."

Well, damn. "How long do dragons live?"

"Oh, ya know, I never bothered to ask. I think Dante is seven hundred and something. So maybe a thousand?"

I shook my head in disbelief. "Sure, a thousand, why not? Follow up question: does Fallon also have a knot?"

In my hand, I felt Alexis pulse. "OK, now we're talking. Spill the beans on dragon dick. Inquiring minds want to know!"

My friend tilted her head and put her hands on her hips. "Knot? On a dick? Tell us about this knot."

"Preferably with imagery, if you can draw," Alexis chimed.

"So that's a no on the Fallon thing. Alright. That means not all shifters have them, I guess," I said.

"I have it on good authority that lamias have two!"

Cin and I looked at the sword in disbelief. "Damn, are these demons just walking around with a surprise box in their pants?" I asked.

"That might be too much for me," Cin confessed, fanning herself. "I'm just not that ambitious. I feel like we need some kind of monster manual for demon dick. If nothing else, just to warn the local woman of what to expect."

Alexis gave off another pulse. "Sweet smoldering iron. If I only had a body, I'd jump on that research task with the speed and tenacity of a wild jungle cat."

"You're a brave gal, I'll give you that," Cin replied.

Down the road, a twig snapped. Immediately, I gripped the sword tighter and held her in front of me. "What was that?"

"What was what?" Cin asked, turning to look at where I was facing.

Her question was met with a pained groan and the sound of shuffling feet. Through the cave of winding trees, a lone figure appeared. The figure was limping something fierce. "Oh gods, please don't let it be another ghoul."

"Shit," Cin cursed. "Brie, come inside with me." She tugged at my arm, but fear had me rooted in place.

The figure dragged itself closer until I could just make out a mop of wild brown hair. "Wait a second." I squinted, trying to get a better look, then waved. "Kitty, is that you?"

The figure straightened and threw a hand up. "Brie? Oh, thank the gods, I finally made it back." Kitty rushed forward toward us, nearly stumbling over her own two feet in the process. I let out a breath of relief when my friend finally came into full view. She looked an absolute mess, but she was alive. Her dark brown curls were half-matted against her head and there were scrapes all over her hands and knees. When Kitty wiped sweat from her brow, I could see ugly black and blue bruises marring her wrists.

I hooked Alexis through my belt and tried to approach her, but Cin held an arm out, stopping me. "Don't," she whispered. "It could just be an illusion."

"Who are you calling an illusion?" Kitty snapped. "Do you have any idea of the raging bullshit I've been through the past few days?"

Cin rolled her eyes, but kept me held back. "It's nothing personal, cuz, just stay there while we sort this out."

Kitty growled and stopped. "How are we going to tell if it's an illusion?" I asked Cin.

A wicked grin spread across her face, and she bent to pick up a pebble. "Sorry Kitty, gotta check!" was all she said before yeeting a pebble at Kitty with zero remorse.

It struck her right in the boob. The disheveled woman let out a yelp and grabbed at her chest. "What the fuck, Cinnamon?" she snarled.

"OK, she's real," Cin chirped. The malicious glint in her eye looked suspiciously similar to her husband's.

Maybe those demons rubbed off on her a little too much. Then again, those two idiots had never really gotten along. If they weren't fighting over the results of a chili competition, it was some other nonsense they felt the need to compete over. I shoved past Cinnamon and went to steady Kitty. The poor girl looked ready to keel over and happily sagged against me when I offered my weight. "Can you tell us what happened?" I asked.

"Yeah." Kitty let out a breath and grabbed hold of my arm. "Out of nowhere this giant deer monster thing grabbed me and—" Blue lightning erupted from her body, encasing us both. Hot streaks of pain raced across my skin in its wake. I screamed and tried to pull away, but some invisible force locked my arms and legs in place. Kitty's eyes had rolled into the back of her head, her mouth had fallen open in a silent scream.

Through a haze of blue and pain, I could see Cinnamon shouting for me. I couldn't answer her. I couldn't do anything. Then the world went black.

Chapter 11

Brie

My head felt like a chew toy for a jaguar. Everything ached, something was dripping on me, it reeked of sweat and sewer, and the world as a whole was just ass. I tried to wipe away the dripping water, only to realize my wrists were bound above my head. Exhaustion weighed on my eyes as I struggled to look around. I blinked, trying to force away the blurry imagery, and damn near fell back asleep.

I squinted, trying to make sense of my surroundings in the dim light. The room was massive and lined with walls made up of big heavy stones. The kind you'd read about in books about castles and fortresses. So this definitely wasn't Boohail. A string of pulsing lights entered my vision. They weaved against the stone walls like a vine, pulsing with a lime green glow. Every six feet, the vine dipped low, then came back up.

Wait... Oh holy shit!

My breath quickened when I noticed that each dip of the vine contained a pair of wrists. Wrists that were *thankfully* still attached to their respective owners. At least twenty figures lined the room. I swung my head up to see the very same vine holding me hostage. When I struggled, the vine wrapped tighter, cutting off my blood flow until I hissed at its sting.

Rough coughing caught my attention. I rolled my heavy head to my left to see Kitty strung up beside me. Her already thin form looked wasted away. Through the tear in her shirt, I could see the outline of her rib cage. Dark bags hung below sunken eyes, and her lips had less moisture than a desert. The woman next to her didn't look any better.

A foot nudged my calf. "Can you stay awake?" a woman whispered.

"Barely," I slurred. My mouth felt like it had been stuffed with cotton. I licked my lips and shifted to look over at her. She looked to be about my age, maybe a bit older. Four braids adorned the side of her head, while the rest of her wild red curls fanned out around her. She didn't look as worn out as the other girls, and the look of unconcealed rage in her black eyes hinted of unspeakable violence.

The red-headed woman nodded toward my feet. "Try to stay focused. Those idiots in red left your sword with you. It's at your feet. Do you think you can maneuver it over to me? The vine holding us is sapping away our energy, so the quicker you move, the better."

"Probably?" Glancing down, I saw Alexis just in front of me. I reached a foot out and tried to nudge her handle closer to me.

"Not yet," the sword hissed. "They're coming back."

"Did that sword just talk?" the redhead asked.

"It's a long story," I sighed.

"Be quiet," the blade hushed again. "They're about to walk in. Pretend to sleep." Her voice was low so as to not alert the owners of the approaching footsteps.

Next to me, the woman went limp and closed her eyes. I stomped down my rising panic and followed suit, letting my body cease all movement.

The wide double doors at the end of the room swung open, and two men in long red cloaks came in. Hoods shielded their faces. The only discernable feature I could make out was that the first one was much shorter than the other. The first man stomped forward, cursing under his breath. He ignored the other women lining the walls and headed straight for me, the second man trailing behind him.

He stopped in front of me and sneered. Green eyes peeked past his hood and he took a moment to check my restraints before cursing again. "Are you sure this is the dragon's wife?" he snarled.

The man behind him clutched at his sleeve. "She should be. Our sources showed that the woman next to her is her kin, and we compelled her to return to the Shadow Dragon's home. Just like you instructed."

Mr. Angry didn't like that response by the way he grit his teeth. "Then tell me why our output hasn't increased?" he snapped, turning to face the taller man. "If she's gained magic from a dragon, then we should have already reached our goal."

The glowing vines and the room full of exhausted women fell together like puzzle pieces in my head. Fallon was right. They're using us to power some kind of spell. And they need Cinnamon. Poor Kitty was just a pawn to get her here, but I ran to her first. That's a relief at least. If they didn't have their key, then there was a chance we could put a stop to whatever they had planned.

Anger Cloak put a hand over his eyes and let out a frustrated sigh. "It's like I have to do everything myself." He snapped his fingers in front of my face. "You. Wake up!"

When I opened my eyes, he continued. "Are you the wife of the Shadow Dragon?"

"Who's asking?"

Pain erupted on the side of my face. I bit the inside of my cheek, refusing to show how much the slap hurt. "I'm asking the questions. Are you the dragon's mate?"

"Don't know any dragons."

Tall Cloak damn near tore his sleeve with his nervous

tugging. "She must be lying! I know we sent the girl to the right house!"

"Dammit Calvin, if she was lying, then where is the dragon magic?" When Calvin remained silent, it was his turn for a slap. The shorter male threw back his hood and rubbed at his temples. Balding dark hair was cropped short against his head.

"Maybe I didn't make myself clear enough," he sighed. "If we don't gain enough magic before the next blood moon, we won't be able to give our god what he needs. You don't want to disappoint him, do you?"

Calvin shook his head.

"Do you know when the next blood moon is?" he asked.

"Three nights from now?" Calvin choked out.

"Three fucking nights! Get me that damned woman or so help me, I will feed you to our master, piece by useless piece!" He slapped him again for good measure and stormed out of the room, slamming the doors behind him.

Calvin slumped to the floor and buried his head in his hands. "Fuck."

"Your boss is a dick," Alexis announced.

"Tell me about it," Calvin sighed. "Wait, who said that?"

"I did."

He looked up from the ground and tilted his head. "A sword?"

"A magic sword!" she chirped. "Why don't you tell your old buddy Alexis what's going on? Maybe we could help each other out."

"Do you know where the dragon's wife is?" he asked, perking up.

"Yes!" she answered brightly. Then fell silent.

"Will…will you tell me?"

"No. I ain't no snitch."

I let out a breath. Relieved that Alexis wasn't willing to sell us out. For now, anyway.

The sword's tone remained light as she spoke. "What do you want with her and these girls, anyway? I've heard of bondage before, but this is extreme. You into some sick shit, Calvin?"

"No!" he shouted, causing a few of the women to stir from their slumber. He stood and waved an arm around the room widely. "These vessels will restore the god Omus to his former glory! With Myva dead and a god on our side, we can establish a new world order." His hood fell back and my stomach lurched at the wild-eyed look on his face.

"I'm sorry, I don't follow."

"Don't you get it?" he rasped. "Myva is dead, and so is her influence. Demons have been freed and are running loose in the streets. People will look for a new church to guide them. With the masses scared and compliant, the Order of The Claw can rise up and set the world right. No longer will men wither away in the shadow of a goddess and her priestesses. We can take our place as true rulers of this world and the women who once scorned us will fall at our feet!"

A dust-covered pause filled the air. "You're doing this because you couldn't get bitches?" Alexis asked.

At my side, the red-headed woman laughed. "I should have known it was a bunch of weak-willed idiots. How pathetic."

His lip curled back in a sneer. "You won't be laughing when—"

"Oh my god, chip my steel, you're so annoying," Alexis snapped. "Maybe if you fixed your attitude and took a bath once in a while, women would talk to you. You smell like old cheese and a mother's regret."

Giggling filled the room as more women woke up. Calvin snapped his head around the room. "Who's laughing?" he roared. "None of you will get any sympathy from me if this is how you behave. We're trying to return you to your natural state as mothers and caregivers."

The redhead shrugged. "We get it, my guy. Mommy said you were special and the girl you liked disagreed. You don't have to join a cult. Maybe get some therapy and aim more in your...you know, looks range."

"You're a bitch," he snapped.

"Mm-mm, tough talk from a guy that just got the shit smacked out of him by a man small enough to fit in my purse," she said, grinning.

Calvin was seething. The bottom half of his face, that was visible, turned several shades of red. "I'll make personally sure you regret—"

Alexis cut him off. "My, you sure love to talk. Ever wonder what it would be like if you stopped?"

He opened his mouth, but the only thing that came out was a sputtering snarl. He turned and trudged out of the room without another word.

"Phew. I thought he'd never leave. OK Brie, try to pick me up again. I might be a little dull, but I should be able to slice through that vine."

"Oh, right." I reached out until my boot brushed against her handle. Carefully, I tried lifting her to my waist, but slipped and the sword clattered to the floor. "Fuck," I hissed.

"Don't get discouraged," the redhead remarked in a cool voice. "That was only the first try. You can do it."

I pursed my lips and tried again. Slowly working the sword up my boots until I could trap the handle between my ankles. "What's your name?" I asked her, looking to fill the silence before I panicked again. Alexis slipped from me and clattered to the floor. "Fuck, fuck!" I grit through clenched teeth and tried again.

"Usha," she replied. "I'm the captain of the *Banshee*. Are you the same Brie that's now mated to Felix?"

"Man, is she ever," Alexis snickered.

"Don't make me drop you again," I snapped. With Alexis' handle firmly grasped, I flipped her to the side, the flat end of the blade facing my ankles. "How does a pirate captain of a demon ship get captured by some cultists? I figured your entourage of orcs would have kept you safe."

She let out a snort and shook her head. "I got into a tiff

with my first mate. He wanted to keep me locked up tighter than a damn prisoner in my own damn ship once we heard lasses were going missing. My temper got the better of me and I stormed off in a huff. Didn't make it halfway across the beach before those freaks snatched me."

Her eyes widened excitedly when I worked the sword higher up my body. "That's it," Usha cheered. "If you can swing her handle up to my mouth, I should be able to cut you down."

I imagined the task would have been a lot easier if I believed in things like exercise and crunches. My stomach screamed with the effort of trying to work the sword up my body. Panting heavily, I held on to the bottom of the blade and rested her hilt on my shoulder. "Are you ready?" I asked Usha.

"Bring it on, lass." With that, I swung my legs up and shifted so Alexis would fall towards Usha. The pommel bonked against her cheek, but the woman recovered and bit down on the handle. She took several deep breaths, then bit down harder and swung her head.

Fear raced down my arms as I felt the blade land just above my fingers. I gulped and looked up to see that the sword had met its mark. "It's only halfway cut. Can you try sawing back and forth?" I asked.

Usha grunted and tried sawing the sword against the magic vine. After a few quick moments, my restraints snapped, and I fell to the floor. Quickly, I took the sword from Usha and cut her down as well. She sighed in relief and clutched her neck.

"I'm gonna need one hell of a tonic after this. My neck is on fire."

"Hey, don't forget about the rest of us," a woman whispered.

We cut the rest of the women down and tried to rouse the ones still sleeping. A few were too weak to stand, but most of the women felt better once they were released from the magic-leeching vine. Kitty, Serena, and Willow were all accounted for. The remaining sixteen claimed to be from the surrounding villages and all had a similar story of being taken in the night by a ghoul or the men in red.

A young petite girl with long black hair tried to stand on wobbly knees, then fell flat on her face. Like Kitty, her face was sunken in and her body wracked with a terrible cough. I knelt down and helped her stand, then was immediately alarmed at how light she was. "What's your name?" I asked.

"Bonnie," she coughed.

"How long have you been here, Bonnie?"

She furrowed her brow and leaned more of her weight against me. "I think at least a week? I'm not sure." Bonnie's eyes became unfocused, and she slumped to the floor. Hot tears spilled down her face. "I don't think I can walk."

I looked at the group of girls, now huddled together like scared ducklings. "You're not the only one," I said.

"Don't leave me here," a blond woman cried.

"Now don't fret. No one's getting left behind," Usha announced. "We'll just have to figure something out, that's all."

"She's right," I began. "Usha, before I was taken, Fallon and Cin were going to send word to your ship about this location. They should be on their way here as we speak. From what Fallon said, they didn't know the extent of the magic user's power and planned to land in the woods just outside of Doncaster and sneak in."

Instead of relief, Usha's face took a serious turn, and she paced back and forth. "Did Cinnamon say she was coming, too?"

"Yes."

"Damn it, of course she is." The redhead bit her thumb and glared at the stone floor.

Serena brushed her brown locks out of her face. "Isn't that a good thing? We just have to wait and be rescued."

Usha's tone was grave. "Not if their goal is to get to Cin. If their new god is anything like Myva, then we need to put a stop to whatever spell they're trying to conjure." She stopped her pacing and pounded a fist in her hand. "Alright, new plan. Anyone who can stand is coming with me. Those who can't, rest here and tear up this vine worse than a rich man's prenup."

"Are you crazy?" Serena asked. "Those cult freaks could kill us."

Usha lifted her chin. "They WILL kill us if we sit still and do nothing. Look at Bonnie." She snapped her fingers at the dark-haired girl. "She looks half dead already. No offense Bonnie."

"No, you're right. I feel like shit."

"Exactly. We can either fight now, or wait until we're weakened and half dead." Usha's voice was commanding. Every bit the pirate captain she mentioned she was. Even though she wasn't the tallest woman in the room, her fierce demeanor made her tower over the rest of us.

"But your friends—"

"Don't know what they're up against," she barked out. "Neither do we. But we stand a better chance of success if we strike from the inside while they attack from the out. Our captors don't know we're free yet and we need to strike before they find out. So I'm going to ask y'all this once. Who can stand?"

Slowly, ten women staggered to their feet. I was already standing, so I just raised my hand. Serena bit her bottom lip and her brow formed a worried crease. "Fuck," she muttered and dragged herself to her feet.

"Lucky thirteen," I whispered. Kitty remained unconscious on the floor, and her friend Willow rested her head on her lap. She gazed up at the women standing, then let her head fall back against the wall. *Guess that's a no from Willow.*

Usha looked at the motley crew and grinned. "Good, that's more of you than I was expecting." She flipped back her long yellow skirts and pulled a dagger off her thigh. "Does anyone else have anything to use as a weapon? And give your names, so I can stop waving blindly at the lot of you."

"Do…do you just keep that on hand?" Serena asked.

Usha cast a deadpan glance at the brunette. "Every woman should carry a weapon."

A dark-skinned, statuesque woman pulled the hairpin from her bun. "This might work." The clasp was that of a raven's skull and the pin was sharp and long. No doubt capable of doing some damage if she aimed correctly. "I'm Lyric, this is my sister, Harmony." She gestured to an identical-looking woman slumped against the wall. Harmony gave us a thumbs up and pulled out a matching hairpin.

Usha nodded in approval and a few more women came forward with knitting needles, another sharp-looking hairpin and an ax. I couldn't help but eye the burly woman who just pulled a full ax out of her skirt. She locked eyes with me and shrugged. "It's my good luck charm. I'm Becca, by the way."

"Never get on her bad side," Alexis whispered.

"Agreed," I replied.

"Alright, ladies," Usha began. "We don't have the luxury of knowing what we're up against or, well, any luxuries really. So I say our best approach is to move quietly and kill anyone we come across before the lot of them realize we've been cut loose. If we follow the vines on the wall, they may just lead us to where the magic is being stored. Once we find it, we smash it to bits. That will give our demon rescue party the best chance at success. Anyone who doesn't have the tits for murder should stay towards the back."

My knees shook with the weight of her words. *I do not know* if my tits were built for murder. I don't even think they were built with my back in mind. The sweat from my palms caused me to lose my grip on Alexis, and I struggled to catch the sword before she fell from my hands.

"Deep breaths, Brie," Alexis whispered. "Try picturing them as giant red peppers. We're just dicing them into a salad. That's all."

I swallowed the lump in my throat and nodded. "Giant red-hot chili peppers. Sure, why not."

Lyric's head snapped towards the door. "Someone's coming."

Usha slunk towards the door and held her knife at the ready. She held a hand up and motioned for the rest of us to line the wall behind her. I steadied my breathing and got into position with the rest of the women. Time slowed to a crawl as the door began to open. A red-cloaked man emerged from the doorway. Before he could even pass the threshold, Usha's dagger was in his neck. His cry was smothered by her hand, and she led the dying man slowly to the floor.

With a grunt, she pulled the blade loose and wiped it off on his cloak. "Let's move."

Numbly, I followed close behind as she led us out the door. The much-needed panic spiral creeping at the edge of my sanity would have to wait. I just hoped Felix and Cin were faring better than us.

Chapter 12

Cinnamon

"Grab his legs!" I shouted, holding on to Felix's neck for dear life. The werewolf thrashed harder. I lost my grip and tumbled straight into a bush. Ignoring the stab of twigs, I hopped up and lunged for him again.

Balabash and Ambrose tried cornering the crazed demon against a large tree. The yellow menace lashed out, damn near gutting Ambrose with sharp claws. "Get out of my way!" he roared.

"You are ruining the sneak attack, you dickhead!" I went to grab at him again, but was foiled by an extremely worn-out-looking Fallon.

My demon took a fistful of my shirt and hoisted me away

from the thrashing werewolf, "Rabbit, there's no talking to him like this. Keep your distance." His words came out in tired slurs. No doubt the consequence of his excessive use of magic. His normally proud features were darkened by rings of purple under his eyes. The hands holding me captive were sluggish, but still immovable for a mere human.

I let out a growl of frustration. Even before we landed, the effects of the love potion had begun to send my friend into a spiraled frenzy. When Felix learned of Brie's capture, he damn near collapsed on the spot. I tried to convince him to stay home. As panicked as he was, I doubted he would be much help in a covert operation. From the looks of his meltdown, I was right.

In order to keep a low profile, the two dragons flew slowly under the cover of a storm cloud. The original plan was to dismount in the forest and have Fallon shroud the area in shadow magic. Most demons had a much better sense of smell and hearing than humans, so picking off the mages would have been a lot easier if they were fighting blind. However, as soon as we landed in the forest outside Doncaster, Felix's eyes glazed over to a hazy red and he tried to run off before anyone else. With the threat of powerful magic users, we had no idea how dangerous the stronghold would be. Not that any of that mattered to a drug-induced love tirade.

With a roar, Felix broke free of Ambrose's hold and darted off towards the fortress in the distance. Three men in red cloaks turned to stare at him, but one met an ill-timed fate beneath the raging claws and desperate fangs. Blood sprayed from the werewolf's maw as he took down every red figure he could find.

Cursing under my breath, I gathered my skirts up and grabbed my bow. "Looks like the surprise attack is over and done with," I hollered to the crew.

Fallon sighed, then pulled himself upright. "I knew we should have knocked him out."

Behind him, Dante lowered himself to the ground and allowed the rest of the demons off his back. When the last passenger jumped off, he shook himself off and leaped back into the air. The silver dragon roared and dark angry clouds spilled into the sky. In seconds, the dragon was engulfed in a raging storm. He shot lightning down below, frying the unfortunate men in red Felix had yet to pick off.

When the angry clouds reached the fortress, they slammed against a lime green force-field. Dante whipped his tail at the barrier, forming a crack in the dome. Cultists rushed along the walls of the keep and began chanting incantations. Immediately, the crack sealed up.

Fallon put a hand on my shoulder and nodded to the other dragon. "Tell the crew to fan out in groups and attack the barrier from as many sections as we can. The more cracks we can form, the faster it comes down. I'm going to support Dante from the air."

"Are you going to be alright if you shift again?" I asked.

He smirked. "It'll take more than this to kill me, Rabbit." Black eyes faded away to warm gold, and my demon stepped away in a shroud of smoke. It swirled upward until a second dragon joined the raging storm.

Wasting no time, I relayed his instructions to the crew of demons, and Serena's crazy-ass mom. Around me, one hundred demons let out bloodthirsty cries, and we descended upon the fort.

Chapter 13

Brie

Staying in the back was a bust. My assailant tried to speak, but was unable to with Alexis embedded in his throat. I reeled back, and he slumped to the floor, dead. My tits were most definitely not built for murder. "Shit."

Usha looked back from the end of the hallway and nodded. "Let's keep moving before more show up," she whispered.

"Well done," Alexis remarked in a low voice. "I didn't even see that guy coming."

"I don't want to be praised for this," I whispered back, catching up to the other women on wobbly knees. The only saving grace of this day is that our captors didn't see it fit to give us water. So I didn't have enough in my bladder to piss myself.

We tiptoed through the keep, following the trail of vines. Their glow grew dimmer with each passing moment and I wondered if the light they gave off was from the magic they sapped from us. If so, then it wouldn't be long before our captors noticed.

At the front of the group, Usha held up a fist and froze. Light flickered at the far end of the hallway and danced around the shadows of two men. She looked around, then ushered us through a door to her left and closed it when the last woman dashed inside.

When my heart stopped beating in my ears, I looked around the dim room to see wall-to-wall shelves lined with glittering pink bottles. Familiar-looking glittering pink bottles. I moved closer and picked one off the shelf. "Oh, you gotta be fucking kidding me."

Harmony shuffled closer to inspect the pink brew. "What is it?"

Anger burned in my gut, but I kept my temper in check to avoid screeching out my rage. "These are the ass-hats that were making love potions," I whispered.

"Wow, these idiots really can't get women on their own," Alexis mused. "Is this whole cult just a cop-out for men who can't talk to women?"

Becca picked up another bottle and read the instructions. "Oh, this does not sit well with me."

Usha scanned the room for any other signs of life, then relaxed. She pocketed her knife and began looking through the walls of potions. "See if you can find a different-colored bottle anywhere. If they have the potion, then they may have the antidote in here too."

Quickly, the group began rummaging through stacks of potions, looking for anything that might free Felix and any other victims from their torment. I pocketed one bottle, just in case we couldn't find the cure. With any luck, Fallon or someone else might be able to find a way to reverse it.

Suddenly, the door creaked open, and a man stepped inside while reading a scroll. He looked up at our group, who immediately froze in place. Wide-eyed, he closed the door.

"Fuck!" Usha cursed. "Grab him!"

Lyric and I dashed after him, damn near taking the door down in our haste. His red cloak billowed behind him, as he sprinted down the hall. "THE WOMEN ARE L—"

A shoe hit him on the back of the head, cutting off his announcement. He stumbled forward and crashed into a wall at the end of the hall.

Lyric hopped on one foot while removing her other shoe. She raised it above her head, ready to fire off her remaining projectile. The man stumbled to his feet and frantically looked down both ends of the hall.

I skittered to a halt in front of him and held the sword to his throat. Swallowing my apprehension, I pressed the blade closer into his skin. "Shout and you die," I grit out. "Now, tell me where you keep the antidote for the love potions."

Sweat rolled down his forehead, and he pushed himself back further against the wall. "Just…just go back to the room you were in and it's kept in the room right next to it."

"Umm…Brie?" Lyric nudged my side. I turned to see her staring towards the top of the staircase.

The wretched stench hit me before I even saw what it was. Icy fear made the hair on my arms stand up as a pair of bloodstained antlers rose from the stairway. I snatched the cloaked man by the collar and dragged him in front of me. "Lyric, get behind us and look down." Her brow furrowed, but she did as instructed. I fished in my pocket for the love potion and threw the sucker as hard as I could at the emerging figure. Then pulled the man's hood down and ducked my head.

The sound of glass shattering, followed by a pained grunt, met my ears. I felt the man tense under my hold. "Wait. What did you just do?" he asked.

"Chad," the ghoul crooned. "I've never noticed how beautiful your eyes are."

"Stay back, beast!" Chad hollered. He twisted out of my hold and backed away from the encroaching monster.

The ghoul spread its twisted limbs wide, the branches along its back cracking with the movement. "Don't run from our love, Chad. We could be so beautiful together."

"Oh, fuck this!" Chad took off, running down the opposite end of the hall, with the monster hot on his heels.

"Come back!" it screeched, sharp claws ticking against the stone floor. "We can open a bed-and-breakfast together!"

When they rounded the corner out of sight, I let out a breath. "Snapping gators. I did not expect that to work." In the distance, Chad let out an earpiercing scream.

Lyric cleared her throat. "Should we...be concerned about him at all?"

"Absolutely not," Alexis stated matter-of-factly.

"Yeah alright. So long as we're all on the same page," she replied, donning her shoes.

Down the hall toward the potion room, I heard Becca shout. The brunette ducked her head out of a room and held a green vial up high. "I found the antidote!" she yelled with a smile. The surrounding women all made shushing noises, and she put a hand to her mouth. "Oh, sorry," she whispered. "I found the antidote."

"Thank goodness," Usha said. She emerged from the same room, holding more vials. She walked over and handed one to me. I pocketed it and gave her my thanks. The pirate captain searched the ceiling for more vines, then pointed down the staircase where the ghoul had come from. "Looks like we're headed deeper into the beast." She held her head up high and scanned the group. "Y'all ready?"

No.

The ground shook with a bang, sending me and most of the other women to the ground. Thunder boomed so loud I felt its vibrations in the stones. I struggled to my feet, then grabbed hold of the wall when the ground shook once more.

"What the hell is that?" I asked.

"That," Usha began, holding her head. "Would be our rescue party. I'm guessing a sneak approach was no longer an option. Alright ladies, our time is up, we gotta move and we gotta move now."

Quickly—well, as quickly as a shaking building would allow—we chased the vines down the spiral staircase and through a grand hall until they disappeared behind gold-plated double doors. Usha set about trying to tug them open.

"Where is everyone?" Harmony asked.

"I imagine it's all hands on deck upstairs," I replied.

"Or not," Alexis chirped.

I turned to ask her what she meant, but my question was answered as the doors were finally pried open. Rows of red-cloaked men kneeled in front of a large pool of water in the center of a courtroom. Their heads bowed in prayer while they raised their clasped hands in front of them. Pulsing vines crept up the walls and across the floor, running in between each praying man until they sank into trunks at each end of the water. Round, egg-like protrusions decorated the trunks. Each pulsed with the same lime green glow from before.

Gross. So gross.

Heads turned to face us, and the mumble of prayer broke. At the front of the group, one man rose up to reassure the others. "Keep praying, my children. Your brothers will need all the magic they can get if we are to repel the scourge on our doorstep," he said, in a soft reassuring voice. He wore the same cloak as the others. The only difference he sported was a long beaded necklace with a pendant shaped like some kind of tail.

"But Father Dave—" A man began to stand, then froze when Father Dave held up his hand.

"I will speak to our guests. Focus on your task."

"Guests?" Usha growled. Her fists clenched. Disdain radiated off her voice like a bull staring down a red cape. "You strung us up and sapped us dry to fuel your weird pool."

Father Dave closed his eyes and held up a hand to her. "Please. Calm yourself." His words did not calm her. If anything, Usha's rage escalated from a bull stomping a hoof to a mama bear baring her teeth in preparation to fuck up everything in the vicinity. The cult leader smiled and cast her a pitying glance. "I assure you, your sacrifices will not be in vain. All my children and I are trying to do is make the world a better place for all mankind."

"Oh, thank goodness!" Alexis let out a loud sigh. "I gotta be honest with ya, Big Daddy Dave. At first I was like, 'Damn, this group looks like they jack off on crystals and kick puppies' and then I saw y'all praying to a glowing puddle. That's when I knew everything was gonna be OK."

His calm demeanor shifted once he realized the origin of the voice. Father Dave sneered at the sword in my hand. A deep red vein popped up on his forehead. "You see?" he shouted. "You've already brought cursed demon magic among us."

"Hey you're no prize either, buddy," Alexis snapped.

"This is unacceptable." He thrashed his arms in our direction and his hood fell back, revealing bloodshot eyes and what was left of a gray head of hair. "Ever since the goddess Myva was destroyed, filthy demons have been pouring into our homes as if they have a right to walk among us. We cannot let this go on. That is why we, the chosen Order of The Claw, will restore order even better than it was before. We won't make the same mistakes that weak goddess made. Under the rule of a TRUE GOD WE WILL—"

An ax flew past my head and landed in Father Dave's shoulder with a sickening thwack. He went down hard, blood spraying from the wound. My mouth fell open, and I looked back to see Becca, with her arm still outstretched.

She looked back at me and shrugged. "What? I saw an opening."

The cult leader writhed on the floor, screaming at his congregants. "Seize them! I want every last drop of magic drained from their bodies!" The surrounding men scrambled to their feet at his words and charged.

Usha stepped in front of me and held her knife at the ready. "Everyone, block Brie and give her an opening to get at those trunks. Our best bet is to destroy the magic at its source."

Oh shit. Why did I have to be the one holding the damn sword?

Harmony and Lyric charged past me. Lyric grabbed the arm of a cultist as he tried to swing and her sister buried her hair pin in his eye. Another man in red went to grab Harmony, but was thwarted by Becca. The stout woman planted her feet and hoisted the man over her shoulder like she was throwing a sack of potatoes.

"Fuck!" Serena's voice came out as a terrified squeak. Yet the woman charged forward all the same.

I jumped when a firm hand grabbed my shoulder. "Let's move!" Usha hollered. We pushed our way toward the other woman. Lyric choked out a cry, and I stabbed at the man with his hands around her neck. He screamed in pain and held the side of his neck. The tall woman recovered quickly and jammed her hairpin into the other side of his neck.

"Summon the ghouls, you idiots!" Father Dave shouted. He staggered to his feet and began dragging himself toward the pool.

Two men broke off from the skirmish and placed their hands on the vines creeping along the floor. The vines lit up like fireflies and sent a wave of pulsing green light down their roots.

"Brie, swing me right!"

I screamed and swung Alexis as hard as I could. Her blade cut into the side of the man about to strike me. Cold sweat and panic fueled my movement, and I thrust her forward, trying to gut another cultist running at us. The room shook just before the blade made contact and the lot of us fell to the floor.

The ceiling cracked, sending down a rain of dust and pebbles. I cursed and jumped up. Trying to make it past our crazy attackers before they could recover. A hand grabbed my leg, and I pitched forward, almost dropping Alexis. Becca recovered her ax from the floor and swung at the offending wrist, cutting it clean off. My stomach rolled at the site of a detached hand still holding on to my ankle.

A putrid reek filled the air, and I heard the loud slam of the doors behind me.

"Shit, we've got company," Alexis cursed. "Better put a pep in that step, Brie." I chanced a glance over my shoulder to see my worst nightmare realized.

Six ghouls burst into the room, followed by even more red-cloaks. Their bone maws clacked together as their claws dragged across the floor. I winced at the horrible screech and ran for all I was worth.

Father Dave had reached the massive pool and was chanting some nonsense into its depths. He caught sight of me and hurled himself at me with a yell. The magic tree trunks were only a few paces away. I tried to pivot past the madman, but he caught the back of my blouse and used his weight to send us both to the floor.

"You insolent little bitch. Did you think I'd let you get in the way of my immortality?" he sneered. He looked at the water and grinned wide, a crazed glint in his eyes.

Grabbing my chin, Father Dave forced me to look into the rising water of the pool. An ear-splitting screech blurred my senses. A gargantuan red creature rose high out of the water until its body almost reached the ceiling. It screeched again, clacking together its claws. Glowing green vines wrapped around its body and dug under its shell.

"Is...is that a damn lobster?" I blinked, trying to see if my eyes were playing tricks on me. Yet the overgrown crustacean remained.

"Bear witness, girl. The almighty Omus will grace this plane once more. With him, the Order of The Claw will gain unlimited power." Father Dave's face turned blotchy in his glee. "If you and your friends were smart, you would have run when you had the chance. Now you'll have the honor of becoming the mighty Omus' first meal."

If one more fucking thing tried to eat me, I was going to burn the world to the ground. Enraged, I dug my fingers into the wound on his shoulder. Father Dave roared in pain and rolled off of me. "The only thing running from you is your hairline," I hissed.

"Brie, stab this balding bitch!" Alexis hollered.

The fort lurched again, sending rocks from the cracked ceiling down around us. Father Dave would have to wait. I wasn't about to be fish food for a damn lobster. The ground shook, and I fought to keep my balance as I darted toward the magic trunks. Aiming Alexis at the first egg-like protrusion, I charged forward into the trunk.

215

Time slowed. Deftly, I registered that I was still holding on to the sword. A far-off grounded part of my mind knew I was still underground in some bullshit cult fortress fighting for my life. But that wasn't what my vision was showing me.

I was underwater. Just an endless sea of water. I tried to grasp at Alexis' hilt, but there was nothing in my hand anymore. There was nothing everywhere, but water. I cried out and my words were swallowed in bubbles. A shiver went up my spine as I felt something move behind me. I whipped around, but saw nothing. Fine hairs brushed along my shoulder blades. My elbow lashed out, connecting with nothing but more water. It was too dark to make out whatever monster was in here with me, but I could have sworn I heard a sigh.

"How disappointing," a voice groaned.

Chapter 14

Brie

The voice came from all directions. In front of me, I could just make out long streaks of thick hair before it swam further into the deep.

"Don't bother looking, child. You won't like what you see."

Dread sank in my belly like a lead weight. "What are you?" I asked, surprised my voice worked again.

The creature hummed. "I haven't been asked that in a long time."

Water rushed beneath my feet. I peered down, only to find an impossible number of eyes looking back at me. I screamed and clawed upward, trying to break the surface of the water.

Laughing, the creature swam further away. "It's no use, child. There is no out. Only here."

"Well, what the fuck is here?" I cried.

The voice took on a somber tone. "It doesn't matter. I don't want to stay long, and you couldn't even if you wanted to." Long tendrils of fine white hair brushed against my ankle. Stinging pain shot across my skin as it skimmed past a minor cut from where that cult member grabbed me.

"It seems those other humans have done you harm." An excited gasp filtered through the water and its tone took on a childlike excitement. "Would you like to punish them?"

I shivered, not liking the gleeful way it said punish. "Aren't you their God, or something?" I stammered.

"I can be."

Damn cryptic disembodied piece of shit. "What the hell does that mean? Either you are or you're not."

"I am power without a body. My old one was taken away, and I was forced back into the ether to survive. If those fools in red were any stronger, I'd already have another body by now." The jelly monster's feelers sank low, as if disappointed. "Alas, good help is so hard to find."

One, two, six, twelve eyes opened a small distance in front of me.

"You're not making any sense," I snarled. "What are you and what do you want?"

Three eyes squinted, as if the creature was grinning. "You."

"What?" Alarm pricked underneath my skin. If it took notice of my distress at its words, the creature gave no indication.

It drifted closer. If I'd eaten earlier that day, there was no doubt in my mind that I would have shat myself. The creature's body somewhat resembled a jellyfish. Its translucent dome-like top ended in a reddish lace. Long white tendrils extended from the top, drifting through the water as if tasting me in the drift. Cloud-like arms as long as an oak tree drifted down past my vision. They folded on top of each other, resembling the frills on a ballgown. Each ruffle ended in an eye. Their irises darted back and forth, looking everywhere at once.

The creature had no mouth from what I could tell, yet it laughed. "Didn't I tell you? You shouldn't have looked."

Too stunned to move, I couldn't answer.

"Answer me, child. The men who hurt you, do you want to get even? I can give you the power to do it. Together, we'll have the power to do anything. Now, doesn't that sound nice?"

I am power without a body. That's what it said. "So you can't survive on your own, is what you're saying? Why didn't you just take over one of the cultists? Also, why a lobster?"

"So many questions," the creature chuckled. "Unfortunately for me, most humans can't sustain my gifts. Even a small glimpse at this form could drive your kind into unspeakable madness. For the past year, I've been stuck in that lesser form, puppeting those idiotic humans into feeding me enough magic just to stay in this realm. Each time I tried to join with one, the fool either disintegrated or fell mad." Long, impossibly soft tendrils drifted along my face. "But you," it rasped. "You can see me just fine, can't you?"

I batted the tendrils away from me. "Why the hell would I want to do that?" I snapped. "Don't tell me you're just another one of those opportunistic ass-hats that thinks they can take over just because Myva was killed?"

Delighted laughter met my ears. "Child, I was Myva."

The white tendrils sifting through the water shot forward and grabbed me. In a flash, I was in a new place. A lush green forest with trees so big around they rivaled the size of my barn. Soft ferns tickled at my waist while moss fought its way across the forest floor. A twig snapped. I whipped around to see a woman walking past me. Her clothes hung off her bony frame like rags and it looked like her long locks hadn't been maintained in a long time. The woman's breath was so labored I thought she might keel over on the spot. Ragged coughs made her stumble, and I reached out a hand to steady her, but it went right through her body.

I followed as she continued on her path until she stopped at the edge of a lake. The woman fell to her knees at the edge of the water and put her forehead to the sand. "Great gods of the deep, if anyone can hear this poor woman's plea, have mercy." Tears spilled down her cheeks and the rest of her prayer was cut off by broken sobs.

"Poor thing," a voice came from the water. "You've been sick for a long time, haven't you?"

"Months." The woman sobbed harder. "Plague has ravaged

my village. Everyone is sick or dead and I can't take the pain any longer. I'll give anything if you just give me relief from this sickness."

White tendrils rose from the water, twisting in the glimmers of harsh sunlight. "I can give you the power to become well again. Agree to host me, child. I'll give you the power to become anything."

Another harsh cough wracked the woman's body until she spat blood. She raised her head and reached out to the offered tendrils. "I accept," she said, before grabbing hold.

A rush of power hit me so strongly, I choked. In an instance, the woman's mind and mine were one and the same. There was a pulse below the skin of our throat where we felt the creature settle into place. Its essence spread down our body like an all-consuming wildfire. We felt better. Our body was no longer ravaged by whatever illness had been plaguing her. As a matter of fact, we felt better than we ever had before.

Memories flitted across my vision. Images of kingdoms falling at my feet, statues sculpted in my likeness. We weren't just better; we were a goddess. The heady feeling of power felt like fine wine against my lips. If we wanted it, we simply took it. Territories, gold, spells, anything.

The memories turned to a demon uprising. Titan creatures, from dragons to giants, launched an all-out assault on one of our castles. It didn't matter what they tried. Anyone would fall at our feet so long as we could perform the right spell.

I knew this story. Everyone did. This was how the goddess Myva saved humanity by sealing all demons behind Volsog gate.

But as the memories flitted past, there were inconsistencies. This Myva…wasn't saving anyone. There was only rage at our city being attacked. It wasn't just demons attacking us, either. Anyone who stood against us was crushed without remorse. It didn't matter how powerful we became; it was never enough. The thrill of gaining even more power was so intoxicating I felt it singing through my blood.

My stomach churned at the sight of our actions. I saw firsthand the lengths Myva went to in order to maintain her control. The children of powerful demons were sacrificed to create a toxin that she could spill from the air, causing all of them to go mad. How blood magic had bound her soul into four chalices so she could fight without being destroyed. How she rewrote the history books to paint herself in a better light, established a religion in her image. Complete with magic-absorbing temples, so her power would only grow.

I pictured Felix and the nightmare of endless darkness he told me about. How he cried out in his sleep.

"Stop!" I screamed. All at once, the array of images ceased, and I was back in the water. My breath came out in ragged pants. Body shaking with rage, I glared at the god, parasite, or whatever the hell it was. "You stay the fuck away from me. I will never host you."

The hundreds of eyes adorning the lower part of its body

all turned toward me. "Don't be foolish, child. Together, we can be anything. I know you felt how good my power can be."

I looked around the water, checking to see if anyone else has appeared in the water. "Psycho! Who is WE? I just told you to stay the fuck away from me."

"So gallant," it mocked. "Don't play coy with me, human. I've lived long enough to watch your species crawl its way out of the sea and take its first pathetic steps on land. No matter how many centuries go by, one thing remains the same." Its white tendrils shot forward and wrapped me up in a tight squeeze. I struggled and tried to fight them away, to no avail. A limb crept up my neck to press against my temple. "Everyone has a price."

A hellish popping noise set off from the tendril wrapped around my head, followed by pain so severe I thought I'd break my own teeth from clenching so hard. More flashes took over my vision. This time, they were my own memories. Tiny bits of my life flitted through the surrounding water. That time I broke my leg falling off a fence, a sleepover at Cinnamon's house, bacon, eggs and toast from last week's breakfast.

Through the agony, I could feel that... Thing, shift through my mind searching for anything of note. "Come now, Brie," it purred. "Just tell me what it is you want most."

Thing paused on a memory of a fight I'd gotten into at a bookstore. I had a blond woman in a headlock while Cherry darted to the counter with the limited edition books we'd snatched away from the raging crowd. We had traveled all the way to Goldcrest City for a massive book fair.

"Knowledge is it?" Thing asked. "Now, this is something we can work with. Tell me, little human, what tomes drove a docile thing like you to violence?"

The memory became clearer in my mind and I let out a laugh. "Now it's your turn not to look."

As expected, the creature shifted closer, forcing deeper into my mind until time skipped to where I was alone with my new purchase. I ran my hands over the discreet cover, admiring the craftsmanship of the filigree carved into the leather binder. Thing's emotions bled into my own. Unabashed, curiosity burned through every fine hair on its tendrils.

I stopped fighting the invasion and relaxed in its hold as past-Me turned the page to read the title. "Plunging Her Briny Depths: A Kraken-Shifter Romance." Confusion marred the ancient parasite's mind. I took it a step further and skipped to where the magic happened in chapter three. Past-Me giggled in her chair, fanning herself. The story's protagonist, Mia, had just given in to her new husband's advances. Her legs spread wide atop his desk, Cassian's gruff beard tickled her neck as he took in her scent. The tentacles coming out of his lower body tore off her dress and plunged mercilessly into her pussy.

Thing shrank back disgusted. The wave of memories ceased for a moment before it recovered and took hold of my mind once more. It said nothing and shifted its focus back to random flits of my life.

"Oh, what's wrong?" I asked. "My reading choices don't make you uncomfortable, do they?"

"Quiet, girl," it growled. "I have no use for your perverse human mating rituals."

Laughing, I steered my thoughts to "Rejected Princess: Book Three." Jolene had been captured by an enemy pack's alpha. "I know just how to make you sing, Princess," Leon whispered into her ear. His sinful mouth explored the curves of her body—

"STOP THAT."

"Oh honey, I'm just getting started." I let out a lewd groan of pleasure and reminisced about my werewolf fucking me within an inch of my life. Felix had me bent over my coffee table and trapped an arm behind my back. My pussy spread for the thick knot at the base of his cock like it was the last shred of physical touch my terminally alone ass was ever going to get.

The creature shuddered and shrank back into the dark water. "What is wrong with you?"

"Oh gods, where do I start?" I tilted my head as if in deep thought. "Hey, do you still want to know what I want? Cause I think I've got something in mind."

"I'm terrified to ask," it groaned.

"Have you ever heard of Omegaverse? If I become your vessel, maybe we can make that a real thing." I clasped my hands together in excitement. "I'll explain the basics to you."

"I don't want that."

"No need to twist my arm about it, I'll tell ya," I chirped, waving the creature off.

"There is a deeply forbidding aura in this water, and it is not coming from me."

Ignoring it, I launched into my explanation. "Alright, so the basics of Omegaverse are alphas, omegas, knotting and, in most cases, mpreg. That's male pregnancy for the uninitiated. Now, omegas go into heat every year once they reach maturity and release an irresistible pheromone that basically drives the alphas into a mating frenzy. That's where the knot comes in." I paused for breath and peeked at the ancient evil. Several of its eyes began twitching in what I could only assume was distress. Doubling down, I began making squelching noises to simulate a particularly wet sex scene I'd read before.

When I grabbed one of its tendrils to send a mental image of an Omegaverse chapter that had illustrations of the couple in question and an oversized riding crop, Thing finally broke. "I can't!" it wailed. "I can't do this."

The world shifted. Water faded away into the pulsing green of the magic trunks and I was back in reality.

"Brie, what the hell are you doing?" Alexis roared. The sword was mere inches from piercing the trunk, her blade vibrated with anticipation. "Stab me into the damn thing already!"

Snapping out of my trance, I shook my head and thrust forward. Burying Alexis into the green egg with a sickening squelch.

Chapter 15

Brie

With a grunt, I dragged Alexis' blade further through the egg protrusion, slicing it wide open, and foul-smelling green liquid spilled out. The sword in question gasped and began to glow as well. Her handle grew hot, and I hissed in pain and let go. I stumbled back to see Alexis levitating in place. The sword let out a gleeful cry and, to my shock, sliced open the rest of the trunk like it was nothing.

"I CAN MOVE!" she cried out. The gargantuan lobster roared in pain as the vines on the right side of its body withered and faded away. Alexis laughed hysterically and plunged herself into the gaping trunk. The green liquid spilling forth. It rose to surround the sword before fading into her. "I CAN

MOVE!" she cried again. "I CAN MOVE AND YOU ARE ALL FUCKED!"

A smidgen of concern worried my brow. *She doesn't mean all of us, right?*

Honestly, it was so hard to tell where that sword stood half the time.

Two ghouls stopped their attempts to drag away Becca and charged at Alexis. The sword let out what I can only describe as maniacal laughter and slashed herself at the brittle deer skull of the one in front. The creature went down hard and the sword whipped herself around to slice the head clean off the second one.

"You hedonistic little bitch!" Father Dave roared. I side-stepped just in time to avoid his punch.

Unarmed, I back away from the larger man. "How are you even still alive?" I asked. The man's shoulder was bleeding profusely and his already pale face was ashen.

Another enraged vein protruded from the side of his head. "You think I'd die at the hands of filthy commoners? I am the savior of this world. The mighty Omus hand-picked me as his anointed one!"

I held up my hands. "Look, I hate to be the one to tell you this, but that thing—" I pointed to the shrieking lobster behind him "—is not Omus. I know it sounds crazy, but you're being manipulated by—"

"SILENCE," he roared. "I will not entertain your lies. I'll kill you myself and string your corpse up so we can drain every last bit of magic from your body." Father Dave shot forward to grab me.

I reared back and tripped over a vine. The madman dove forward and wrapped his hands around my neck. I choked and clawed at his hands, trying to buck him off.

Air flooded my lungs as Father Dave was knocked off me. I gasped, taking in big gulps of air, then turned to see Felix.

The werewolf raked his claws down the screaming anointed one's torso. Felix bit into his neck and the screaming cut short.

"Oh thank the gods." I struggled to my feet and called out to him. But he ignored me in favor of continuously tearing away at the dead man. "Um…hon? I think you got him."

Finally, the werewolf snapped his head in my direction. The crazed, rabid eyes of a feral dog pinned me in place like a lamb to the slaughter. It wasn't until he stepped closer that I noticed the frantic beat of his heart. *Shit, shit, shit.* The love potion must have been driving him mad in my absence. Slowly, I reached into my pocket and grabbed the antidote.

Felix snarled and prowled closer to me. Blood dripped from his maw and the kind eyes I'd come to know were gone without a trace. Around the room, I could hear the fight continuing. More demons spilled into the courtroom and attacked the ghouls head on. Yet none of them were close enough to stop him should he decide to gut me next. My knees shook, and I tried to keep my voice as calm as possible. "Felix, love? Do you know who I am?"

His answer was a menacing growl.

"Is that 'grrr, yes I love you. Run away with me, light of my life'?" I brought the vial to my mouth and bit off the cork. "This is the antidote for the love potion," I told him gently. "I'm just going to come a little closer and dump this down your throat, OK? Don't eat me."

The werewolf bristled. "No."

"No?" I parroted back at him. "Why no?" Slowly, I edged a little closer. I only had one vial and I couldn't risk him dodging my throw.

Felix snarled and shook his head wildly. His voice came in the form of a menacing snarl, "No one is taking you from me."

"I'm literally right here. Just hold still."

His eyes widened when I raised the vial higher. "No," he barked out. "You'll leave if I lose this love potion. You can't leave." His words came out faster, and he clawed at his head before shaking frantically.

I'm not the one forced to be in love. A selfish part of me was terrified of what would happen once Felix was freed from his curse. The days we spent together had become so unbelievably precious. I couldn't remember a time when I connected so strongly with another person. The thought of Felix simply getting up and walking away from me now had my heart squeezing in my chest. But if it wasn't real, then I couldn't hold him hostage. No one deserves to have their choices taken away from them. If I didn't do this now, then I'd be no better than the cultists.

"You can't," he snapped, desperation palpable in his voice.

Before I could even blink, Felix lunged forward and sank his fangs into my arm. I cried out as we hit the ground, and quickly held my thumb over the top of the vial so it wouldn't spill. Felix kept me pinned underneath him, his body wracked with the tremors of his overworked heart. Ignoring the pain in my arm, I dumped the vial over his head.

The response was almost instant. Felix's body relaxed and the cacophony of his heartbeat silenced. I remained completely still, waiting for my husband to fully come to his senses. Slowly, he let go of my arm. I bit my lip and tried not to cry out at the throbbing pain.

Horror crossed his face as he looked down at the bite wound. "Brie. Oh gods, what have I done?"

I smiled up at him. "It doesn't hurt that much." *Lies! It hurts so bad.* "You can make it up to me later, alright?" I gestured to the all-out brawl happening around us. "We're still in a bit of a situation here."

His eyes searched mine. He opened his mouth to speak, then shut it again.

I gave his arm a gentle squeeze. "Later," I said.

Felix's ears flattened, but he nodded and helped me up. "Just stay here. I'll come get you when it's over."

The ground pitched, and suddenly most of the ceiling was ripped clean off the fortress. A silver dragon dug his claws into the remaining stone and then paused, tilting his massive head. "Is that a giant lobster?"

The battle came to a halt. The remaining cultists didn't strike me as a rather intelligent lot, but there wasn't much to be done when two dragons and a small army of demons started tearing holes in your keep. Just to make sure we left nothing up to question, I had Fallon and Dante "not Dillon" burn every last bit of the vines to a crisp.

Cinnamon crushed me to her as soon as she burst into the room and immediately ruined my shirt with her snot and tears. In between her sobbing and hiccups, she still managed to say the most Cinnamon thing I've ever heard in my life. "So like, we can eat that lobster, right?"

I sighed and eased my injured arm away from her crushing hug. "I guess it would make one hell of a celebratory feast."

"At the beach?"

Cin and I jumped at the sudden voice next to us. Alexis' blade had turned blood orange, and I really hoped that was because of the magic she absorbed and not the endless amount of blood I was sure she'd sliced through. "I mean, I'm kinda scared to tell you no, so yeah, sure. We can have the party at the beach," I said.

"Your fear is both noted and appreciated!" the sword said with glee.

Cin released me from her death grip and eyed Alexis. "Holy shit, you can float!"

In response, the blade gave off a pulse of bright orange light. "Float, move, murder. It's been a big day for me."

Chapter 16

Brie

That fucker was ignoring me. I stabbed my fork into my lobster mac 'n' cheese and took a bite. Dammit all. It was so good. Even my anger wasn't enough to taint the magic of Mrs. Hotpepper's lobster mac recipe.

Puffer Cove was alive with music, good food, and good times. Every stolen woman was alive and accounted for, and there was enough lobster to go around for days. Yet I couldn't shake the feeling of dread in my chest. Felix hadn't spoken to me since we returned to Boohail that morning.

At my side, Usha rolled her eyes and sipped her mead. "Just go find him, ya pissy thing."

"I am not being pissy."

She snorted. "You showed that cult leader more mercy than the innocent plate you're stabbing."

I sighed and scanned the crowd, looking for a familiar mop of blond hair. "If it's so easy, then why are you hiding next to me instead of joining the party?"

Usha picked a sizable chunk of lobster meat from her plate and tossed it to the hyena at her side. The beast caught the treat mid-air, then lay down next to her master. "If one more of my men hugs me or asks if I'm alright, I'll be the one tearing off limbs."

"If you say so." I was positive it had something to do with the handsome lamia she was clearly avoiding, but I didn't want her prying into my issues either. So I kept my mouth shut. I took a deep breath and set my plate down on a nearby rock. "You're right," I told her.

"I know," she mused. "I usually am. It's a wonder more people don't just listen the first time." The redhead dug her fork into my plate and helped herself. "Find Dante. Felix is usually bothering the shit out of him."

I made my way through the crowd of party-goers, determined to find Felix or his silver-haired companion. Humans and demons alike were dancing around a bonfire while Alexis was flying around nearby. Conveniently at butt level.

Thankfully, Dante wasn't hard to find. He and Fallon were pretty much the only men in Boohail over seven feet tall, so really, you just needed to look up. The dragon shifter was bent near the cooking station with Cinnamon and Kitty. He looked utterly distraught as my two favorite idiots gave him conflicting instructions about how to properly season a lobster bisque.

"You can't just dump a handful of cayenne in there. You'll overpower the rest of the bisque, you overzealous twat," Cin scolded.

Kitty crossed her arms and glared at her cousin. "And once again, you're wrong. That lobster is huge. Everybody knows that the smaller lobsters taste better. So we're going to have to overcompensate with spices if we want this to turn out right."

Cin growled in frustration. "You don't make a lobster bisque for the flavor of a lobster itself. It tastes like butter, cream and goodness. The lobster comes in for the texture and light flavoring. It's a TEXTURE DISH!"

"Dante, have you seen Felix?" I asked, ignoring the other two.

The man looked relieved for the excuse to step away. "Yes," he said, ushering us away from the table. "He asked me if I knew anything about curse removals. I have an old book on it in my quarters, so I sent him there."

"Curse removal? He just got his removed."

Dante nodded towards my arm. "I don't think he was talking about his curse."

I looked at my bandaged arm, then realization dawned. Felix bit me. I was going to turn into a werewolf. Which should have made him happy...if I really was his fated mate.

"Oh, well thanks, Dante, I'll go find him." The dragon shifter nodded and headed back into the crowd.

Numbly, I ventured out of the cove, bypassing the shipyard, and headed home. Felix didn't love me anymore. That was the only explanation. Hot tears filled my eyes, and I furiously wiped them away. I wasn't the type of bitch to cry in public, and I would not start now. Walking faster, I ignored the gaggle of villagers heading to the party and went straight home.

Seeing the shiny new Monet name plate resting proudly against my roses was an extra punch to the gut. Hurt, I snatched the plate off its hanger and threw it as hard as I could into the woods.

Once inside, I kicked off my shoes and went straight for my liquor cabinet. Only to realize Felix was sitting in the living room. A large book was spread out before him, along with a notepad full of scribbles. The blond was so focused on his reading that he didn't even notice me come in. I'd never seen the man so serious. His playful smile had vanished under a firm line, and his brow was pulled tight into a crease. Yet he still managed to drape himself comfortably on my couch as if he lived here with me for years. As if this was still our home.

Fuck, I loved him. I loved him so much and he didn't even have the decency to tell me straight up I wasn't his fated mate. "What are you doing here?" I asked, trying to keep my voice from breaking.

Finally, he looked up from his book. "Brie."

Brie, not Lamb.

"Answer my question. What are you doing here, Felix?"

He looked around confused, then tilted his head. "I... live here?"

He put the book down and came to me. Brushing his thumb over my shoulder as if I were a porcelain doll that would break if he did anything else. "I know you must be angry. You have every right to be after what I've done. But I'm sure I can find a cure for you before you shift on the next full moon. We have almost a full month to sort this out."

I closed my eyes, so I wouldn't get lost in his. "Isn't there something else you want to tell me?"

His body tensed. "Yes," he said gravely. "Brie, I am so sorry for biting you. I was out of my mind with need and—"

"Not that," I snapped. "I don't care about some stupid bite."

"You...you don't?"

I swatted his hands and stepped away. My heart felt like lead in my chest. I wanted nothing more than to bury myself in the hole of my self-pity and forget the world.

"I know why you're trying to stop me from becoming a werewolf. Just tell me I'm not your fated mate and get out. I already told you I wouldn't hold it against you if things didn't turn out the way we wanted."

Even with my back to him, his gaze seared into my flesh,

piercing through every wall I'd ever been bothered to put up, until they lay in a crumpled heap at my feet.

"Brie," he whispered.

"Stop calling me that," I bit out, losing the fight against my tears.

Turning to face him, I did my best to keep my head high. "I'm a grown woman. I can handle the truth. Just spit it out."

I yelped when Felix suddenly reached out and crushed me to him. He buried his face in the crown of my hair and inhaled deeply. His voice came out in an agonized growl. "Of course you're my fated mate. I told you that from day one."

"I…But you're trying to break the curse before I turn."

"Love, I bit you without permission. Ever since I laid eyes on you, I've been on a mission to earn your love and prove to you I wasn't the monster you saw in the woods. And yet that is exactly what I proved to you, when I acted no better than a feral beast. I never wanted to take the choice from you. But dammit, Lamb—when I came into the room and saw that man's hands around your throat…" He paused, the hands wrapped so tightly around my body filled with tremors. "… the only thing that mattered was his death and your safety. It didn't matter if I had to turn you to make that happen. If becoming a werewolf would have given you the strength to survive that encounter, I would have done it a thousand times over. Hate me if you want. You're not allowed to get hurt, you know. I can't bear it."

I sniffed and returned his embrace. "Then you're never allowed to ignore me like that again. I thought I lost you."

Felix let out a shaky laugh and a furious rush of joy warmed my skin as I felt his smile against my temple. "As if you could ever be rid of me."

"Well," I said, patting his chest and leaning away from him, "if you'll excuse me for a moment, I need to go find our nameplate."

Felix wiped a tear from my face and smiled softly. His face was reminiscent of the sun—staring at it for too long was tear-inducing, but unmistakably magnificent. "What happened to the nameplate?"

My mouth quirked, and I stroked my fingers over the masculine bridge of his collarbone. "I may have…thrown it into the woods."

He gripped the back of my head and let his lips trace against my own. His other hand pressed against the small of my back until I was flush against him. "You're so cute when you're mad."

I brushed my lips against his. Drinking in his nearness like water in a drought. "I love you."

His breath hitched. "Say it again."

"I love you, Felix."

He cursed under his breath. "Sweetheart, I'm afraid I may have lost some of my hearing in the battle. Say it one more time."

I ran my fingers through his soft hair and kissed him. "I'll repeat it as many times as you need me to."

Felix shuddered and ran his hand down my back to grip my ass, before nipping playfully at my lip. "Be careful what you say to me, Lamb."

Epilogue

Dante

Waves rocked across my back in a slow, soothing rhythm. A ray of sun peeked out of the clouds, just wide enough to shine down and warm my scales. I burrowed a little deeper into the sand and let the soft warmth cushion my weight. In the distance, rolling thunder beat against gray skies. Not close enough to be too loud, but just right. My head lolled against the warm beach of Puffer Cove and I let out a sigh of contentment.

With the previous night's celebration over and done with, my makeshift bed was finally free of intruders. It wasn't as good as the bed that I had painstakingly crafted back in my castle in Volsog, but it was damn close. My eyelids grew heavy with the sweet promise of sleep lulling my senses.

The sound of crashing footsteps ruined my precious ocean symphony. I shut my eyes tighter, hoping whoever it was passed by quickly.

"DANTE," an all-too-familiar voice screamed.

Not this fucking guy.

A blur of yellow fur bounded into my peaceful cove, leaving paw prints in my previously perfect sand. Felix called out again before tripping over a log in his haste. He shielded a blanket-wrapped package as he went down, and scrambled back onto his feet.

I wonder how much fur I'd have to pick out of my teeth if I just ate him.

"Dante, I need your help," he panted, skidding to a halt in front of me.

"No."

"Come on," he whined. "You're not even busy."

"I'm very busy," I bit out. **"I'm debating whether my nap would be worth the hairball I'd get from eating you."**

The werewolf rolled his eyes. "Don't be dramatic. I'm your best friend."

"I don't recall ever agreeing to that," I sighed.

"We're best friends," he nodded. "Besides, I brought pies." He set a blanket-wrapped basket down and smiled. "I just need you to take the birth control rune off. Now. Right now."

"I don't see how this couldn't wait until I was awake."

Felix cast me a pitying glance. "Don't worry Dante, one day

you'll have a mate of your own and understand the importance of *urgency*." The last of his words came out in an impatient snarl. "Rune. Off. Now. Thank you."

The distant thunder let off an impressive boom. "**I don't feel like it right now,**" I said, stretching out a little further in the sand.

His tail twitched. "Look, best friend—"

"**Not your best friend.**"

"Brother, confidante, comrade, boon companion. You might want to start being a little nicer to me when it comes to matters of the heart."

I scoffed. "**Please, O wise one, enlighten me as to why?**"

"You plan on finding a mate of your own soon, don't you?"

"**Obviously.**"

I couldn't think of one demon who didn't have plans of his own female one day. One of the biggest advantages of traveling to Boohail was to see if anyone else would have Fallon's luck of finding a mate here. Unfortunately for me, that didn't pan out. But the food was good, and I liked my cove.

Felix hummed and nodded. "Good, good. Follow up question: when's the last time you actually spoke to a human woman? No, Cinnamon and Usha don't count. Those two are a special breed, all their own."

I thought for a moment. "**Alexis.**"

"Is a sword," he retorted.

"**What's your point?**" I growled.

"My point is," he began, "human women aren't like demon women. They don't care if you're a powerful dragon. They don't even imprint. So you're going to have to actually speak to her and let's be honest here, niceties are not your strong point. And because I'm such an excellent boon companion, I am willing to help you when you inevitably piss her off." He leaned forward and lowered his voice. "And you will piss her off."

A pregnant pause filled the air as I stared at him. **"There better be lemon meringue pie in that basket."**

"Lemon, peanut butter, pecan, the works." He pointed to the small rune buried under his fur. "Let's go, bud."

Sighing, I sent a small jolt of magic at the rune to dispel it. The sealing magic fizzled and popped and the little M shape faded away. **"Alright, go, and leave the basket. I'm trying to sleep."**

Felix's face broke into a wide grin and he turned tail and bolted from the cove. "I'm going to be a dad," he yelled into the winds.

Despite myself, a small tinge of jealousy wormed its way into my chest as I watched him go. Fallon and Felix had both found their mates. Something only a small few of us could dream of a year ago. But now anything was possible. And my female could be out there.

Mind made up, I stretched back in the sand. Tomorrow, I'd bid Usha and the rest of the crew farewell and begin my search. But not today. Today was for sleep.

The story continues in...

THAT TIME I GOT DRUNK AND

SAVED A HUMAN

Book THREE of the Mead Mishaps series

Acknowledgments

Whoever invented crème brûlée coffee. All my readers who took a chance on my debut novel and followed me on this journey. This wouldn't have happened without you.

Also my family and friends. Obviously.

extras

orbit

meet the author

Kimberly Lemming

KIMBERLY LEMMING is on an eternal quest to avoid her calling as a main character. She can be found giving the slip to that new werewolf that just blew into town and refusing to make eye contact with a prince of a far-off land. Dodging aliens looking for Earth booty can really take up a girl's time. But when she's not running from fate, she can be found writing diverse fantasy romance. Or just shoveling chocolate in her maw until she passes out on the couch.

Find out more about Kimberly Lemming and other Orbit authors by registering for the free monthly newsletter at orbitbooks.net.

if you enjoyed

THAT TIME I GOT DRUNK AND YEETED A LOVE POTION AT A WEREWOLF

look out for

HALF A SOUL

Regency Faerie Tales: Book One

by

Olivia Atwater

It's difficult to find a husband in Regency England when you're a young lady with only half a soul.

Ever since she was cursed by a faerie, Theodora Ettings has had no sense of fear or embarrassment—an unfortunate condition that leaves her prone to accidental scandal. Dora hopes to be a quiet, sensible wallflower during the London

Season—but when Elias Wilder, the handsome, peculiar, and utterly ill-mannered Lord Sorcier, discovers her condition, she is instead drawn into strange and dangerous faerie affairs.

If her reputation can survive both her curse and her sudden connection with the least liked man in all high society, then she and her family may yet reclaim their normal place in the world. But the longer Dora spends with Elias, the more she begins to suspect that one may indeed fall in love even with only half a soul.

Chapter One

Sir Albus Balfour was nattering on about his family's horses again.

Now, to be clear, Dora *liked* horses. She didn't mind the occasional discussion on the subject of equine family trees. But Sir Albus had the most singular way of draining all normal sustenance from a conversation with his monotonous voice and his insistence on drawing out the first syllable in the word *pure*bred. By Dora's admittedly distracted count, in fact, Sir Albus had used the word *pure*bred nearly a hundred times since she and Vanessa had first arrived at Lady Walcote's dratted garden party.

Poor Vanessa. She had finally come out into society at eighteen years old – and already she found herself surrounded by suitors of the worst sort. Her luscious golden hair, her fair, unfreckled complexion and her utterly sweet demeanour had so far attracted every scoundrel, gambler and toothless old man within the county. Surely Dora's lovely cousin would be equally attractive to far better suitors… but Dora greatly suspected that such men were out in London, if they were to be found anywhere at all.

At nineteen – very nearly pushing twenty! – Dora was on the verge of being considered a spinster, though she had supposedly entered society alongside her cousin. In reality, Dora knew that Vanessa had only put off her own debut for so long in order to keep her company. No one in the family was under any illusions as to Dora's attractiveness to potential suitors, with her one strange eye and her bizarre demeanour.

"Have you ever wondered what might happen if we bred a horse with a dolphin, Sir Albus?" Dora interrupted distantly.

"I— What?" The older fellow blinked, caught off his stride by the unexpected question. His salt-and-pepper moustache twitched, and the wrinkles at the corners of his eyes deepened, perplexed. "No, I cannot say that I have, Miss Ettings. The two simply do not mix." He seemed at a loss that he even had to explain the second part. Sir Albus turned his attention instantly back towards Vanessa. "Now, as I was saying, the mare was *pure*bred, but she wasn't to be of any use unless we could find an equally impressive stud—"

Vanessa winced imperceptibly at the repetition of the word *pure*bred. Aha. So she *had* noticed the awful pattern.

Dora interrupted again.

"—but do you think such a union would produce a dolphin's head and a horse's end, or do you think it would be the other way around?" she asked Sir Albus in a bemused tone.

Sir Albus shot Dora a venomous look. "Now see here," he began.

"Oh, what a fun thought!" Vanessa said, with desperate cheer. "You do always come up with the most wonderful games, Dora!" Vanessa looped her arm through Dora's, squeezing at her elbow a bit more firmly than was necessary, then turned her eyes back towards Sir Albus. "Might we inquire as to your expert opinion, sir?" she asked. "Which would it be, do you think?"

Sir Albus flailed at this, flustered out of his rhythm. He had only one script, Dora observed idly, and absolutely no imagination with which to deviate from it. "I...I could not possibly answer such an absurd question!" he managed. "The very idea! It's impossible!"

"Oh, but I'm sure that the Lord Sorcier would know," Dora observed to Vanessa. Her thoughts meandered slowly away from the subject, and on to other matters. "I hear the new court magician is quite talented. He defeated Napoleon's Lord Sorcier at Vitoria, you know. He does at least three impossible things before breakfast, the way I hear it told. Certainly, *he* could tell us which end would be which."

Vanessa blinked at that for some reason, as though Dora had revealed a great secret to her instead of a bit of idle gossip. "Well," Vanessa said slowly, "the Lord Sorcier is almost certainly in London, far away from here. And I wonder if he would lower himself to answering such a question, even if it *were* the sort of impossible thing he could accomplish." Vanessa cleared her throat and turned her eyes to the rest of the garden party. "But perhaps there are some here with a less *impossible* grasp of magic who might offer their expert opinion instead?"

Sir Albus's moustache was all but vibrating now, as he failed to suppress his outrage at the conversation's turn away from him and his prized horses. "Young lady!" he sputtered towards Dora. "That is *quite* enough! If you wish to discuss flights of fancy, then please do so somewhere far afield from us. We are having a serious, adult conversation!"

The man's vehemence was such that a drop of spittle hit Dora along the cheek. She blinked at him slowly. Sir Albus was red-faced and shaking with upset, leaning towards her in a vaguely threatening manner. Dimly, Dora knew she *ought* to be afraid of him – any other lady might have cringed back from such a violent outpouring of passion. But whatever impulse normally made ladies wither and faint in the face of frightening things had been lost on its way to her conscious mind for years on end now.

"Sir!" Vanessa managed in a shocked, trembling voice. "You must not address my cousin in such a way. Such behaviour is absolutely beyond the pale!"

Dora glanced towards her cousin, considering the way that her lip trembled and her hands clutched together. Quietly, she tried to mirror the gestures. Her aunt had begged her to act *normal* at this party, after all.

For a moment, as Dora turned her trembling lip back towards Sir Albus, a chastised look crossed his eyes. "I...I do apologise," he said stiffly. But Dora noticed that he addressed the apology to Vanessa, and not to her.

"Apologise for what?" Dora murmured absently. "For impacting your chances with my cousin, or for acting the boor?"

Sir Albus widened his eyes in shocked fury.

Oh, Dora thought with a sigh. *That was not the sort of thing that normal, frightened women say, I suppose.*

"Your apology is accepted!" Vanessa blurted out quickly. She pushed to her feet as she spoke, dragging Dora firmly away by the arm. "But I...I'm afraid I must go and regain my composure, sir. We shall have to discuss this further at another time."

Vanessa charged for the house with as much ladylike delicacy as she could muster while hauling her older cousin behind her.

"I've fumbled things again, haven't I?" Dora asked her softly. A distant pang of distress clenched at her heart. Acute problems rarely seemed to trouble Dora the way that they should, but emotions born of longer, wearier issues still hung upon her like a shroud. *Vanessa should be married by now*, Dora thought. *She would be married if not for me.* It was an old idea by now, and it never failed to sadden her.

"Oh no, you haven't at all!" Vanessa reassured her cousin as they slipped inside the house. "You've saved me again, Dora. Perhaps you were a bit pert, but I don't know if I could have stood to listen to him say that word even one more time!"

"What, *pure*bred?" Dora asked, with a faint curve of her lips.

Vanessa shuddered. "Oh, please don't," she said. "It's just awful. I'll never be able to listen to anyone talk about horses again without hearing it that way."

Dora smiled gently back at her. Though Dora's soul was numb and distant, her cousin's presence remained a warm and steady light beside her. Vanessa was like a glowing lantern in the dark, or a comforting fire in the hearth. Dora had no joy of her own – though she knew the sense of contentment, or a kind of pleasant peace. But when Vanessa was happy, Dora sometimes swore she could feel it rubbing off on her, seeping into the holes where her own happiness had once been torn away and lighting a little lantern of her own.

"I don't think you would have enjoyed marrying him anyway," Dora told Vanessa. "Though I'll be sad if I've scared away some other man you would have liked more."

Vanessa sighed heavily. "I don't intend to marry and leave you all alone, Dora," she said quietly. "I really worry that Mother might turn you out entirely if I wasn't there to insist otherwise." Her lips turned down into a troubled frown that was still somehow prettier than any smile had ever looked on Dora's face. "But if I *must* marry, I should hope that it would be a man who didn't mind you coming to live with me."

"That is a very difficult thing to ask," Dora chided Vanessa, though the words touched gently at that warm, ember glow within her. "Few men will wish to share their new wife with some mad cousin who wears embroidery scissors around her neck."

Vanessa's eyes glanced towards the top of Dora's dress. They both knew of the little leather sheath that pressed against her breast, still carrying those iron scissors. It had been Vanessa's idea. *Lord Hollowvale fears those scissors,* she had said, *so you should have them on you always, in case he comes for you and I am not around to stab him in his other leg.*

Vanessa pursed her lips. "Well!" she said. "I suppose I shall have to be difficult, then. For the only way I shall ever be parted from you, Dora, is if you become mad with love and desert me for some wonderful husband of your own." Her eyes brightened at the thought. "Wouldn't it be wonderful if we fell in love at the same time? I could go to your wedding, then, and you could come to mine!"

Dora smiled placidly at her cousin. *No one is ever going to marry me,* she thought. But she didn't say it aloud. The thought was barely a nuisance – rather like that fly in the corner – but Vanessa was always so horrified when Dora said common sense things like that. Dora didn't like upsetting Vanessa, so she kept the thought to herself. "That would be very nice," she said instead.

Vanessa chewed at her lower lip, and Dora wondered whether her cousin had somehow guessed her thoughts.

"…either way," Vanessa said finally, "neither of us shall find a proper husband in the country, I think. Mother has been bothering me to go to London for the Season, you know. I believe I want to go, Dora – but only if you swear you will come with me."

Dora blinked at her cousin slowly. *Auntie Frances will not like that at all,* she thought. But Vanessa, for all of her lovely grace and charm and good behaviour, always did seem to get her way with her stern-eyed mother.

On the one hand, Dora thought, she was quite certain that she would be just as much a hindrance to Vanessa's marriage prospects in London as she was here in the country. But on the other hand, there were bound to be any number of Sir Albuses hunting about London's ballrooms as well, just waiting to pounce on her poor, good-natured cousin. And as much of a terror as Vanessa was to faerie gentry, she really was as meek as a mouse when it came to normal human beings.

"I suppose I must come with you, then," Dora agreed. "If only so you needn't talk of horses ever again."

Vanessa smiled winsomely at her. "You are my hero, Dora," she said.

That lantern light within Dora glowed a tiny bit brighter at the words. "But you were mine first," she replied. "So I must certainly repay the debt."

Vanessa took her by the arm again – and soon Dora's thoughts had wandered well away from London, and far afield from things like purebred horses and impossible court magicians.

Auntie Frances was *not* pleased at the idea of Dora accompanying her cousin to London. "She'll require dresses!" was the woman's very first protest, as they discussed the matter over tea. "It will be far too expensive to dress two of you! I am sure that Lord Lockheed will not approve the money."

"She can wear my old dresses," Vanessa replied cheerfully, as though she'd already thought this through. "You always did like the pink muslin, didn't you, Dora?" Dora, for her part, merely nodded along obligingly and sipped at her teacup.

"She'll drive away your suitors!" Auntie Frances sputtered next. "What with her *strangeness*—"

"Mother!" Vanessa protested, with a glance at Dora. "Must you speak so awfully? And right in front of her as well!"

Auntie Frances frowned darkly. "She doesn't *care*, Vanessa," she said shortly. "Look at her. Getting that girl to feel anything at all is an exercise in futility. She may as well be a doll you carry around with you for comfort."

Dora sipped at her tea again, unfazed. The words failed to prick at her in the way that they should have. She wasn't upset or offended or tempted to weep. There was a small part of her, however – very deep down – that added the comment to a longstanding pile of other, similar comments. That pile gave her a faint sinking feeling which she never could quite shake. Sometimes, she would find herself taking it out and examining it in the middle of the night, for no particular reason she could discern.

Vanessa, however, was quite visibly crushed. Her eyes filled up with tears. "You can't mean that, Mother," she said. "Oh, *please* take it back! I shan't be able to forgive you if you won't!"

Auntie Frances stiffened her posture at her daughter's obvious misery. A weary resignation flickered across her features. "Yes, *fine*," she sighed, though she didn't look at Dora as she said it. "That comment was somewhat over the line." She pulled out her lace handkerchief and handed it over to her daughter. "Do you really wish to go to London, Dora?" she asked. It was clear from her tone that she expected to hear some vague, noncommittal answer.

"I do," Dora told her serenely. Auntie Frances frowned sharply at that and glanced towards her.

Because Vanessa wants me there, Dora thought. *And I don't want to leave her.* But she thought that this elaboration might complicate the point, and so she kept it to herself.

extras

Auntie Frances said that she would think on the matter. Dora suspected that this was her way of delaying the conversation and hoping that Vanessa would change her mind.

But Vanessa Ettings always did get her way eventually.

Thus it was that they soon took off for London, all three of them. Lord Lockheed, always distant and more consumed with his affairs than with his daughter, did not deign to accompany them – but Auntie Frances had pulled strings through her sister's husband to secure them a place to stay with the Countess of Hayworth, who was possessed of a residence within London and only too pleased to have guests. Since Vanessa had declared her interest so belatedly, they had to wait for the roads to clear of mud – by the time they left Lockheed for London, it was already late March, with only a month or two left in the Season.

After so much fuss, the carriage into London was not at all how Dora might have imagined it. Even in her usual detached state, she couldn't help but notice the stench as they entered the city proper. It was a rude mixture of sweat, urine and other things, all packed together in too close a space. Auntie Frances and Vanessa reacted much more visibly; Auntie Frances pulled out her handkerchief and pressed it over her mouth, while Vanessa knit her brow and craned her head to look outside the carriage. Dora followed Vanessa's lead, glancing over her cousin's shoulder to see out the window.

There were so very *many* people. It was one thing to be told that London was well-populated, and another thing entirely to see it with one's own eyes. All those people running back and forth in the street got into each other's way, and they all seemed somewhat cross with one another. Often, their driver had to yell at someone crossing in front of their carriage, shaking his fist and threatening to run them down.

The noise would have been startling, if Dora were capable of being startled. It settled into her bones more readily than anything else had ever done, however – the biggest fly yet in the corner of the room. Dora found herself frowning at the chaos.

Thankfully, both the hubbub and the awful scents died down as their carriage crossed further into the city, onto wider, calmer avenues. The jumble of buildings that passed them slowly became more elegant and refined, and the suffocating press of people thinned out. Eventually, their carriage driver stopped them in front of a tall, terraced townhouse and stepped down to open the doors for them.

The front door of the townhouse opened just as Dora was stepping down after her cousin and her aunt. A maid and a footman both exited, followed by a thin, steel-haired woman in a dignified rose and beige gown. The two servants swept past, already helping to unload their things, while the older woman stepped out with a smile and took Auntie Frances's hands in hers.

"My dear Lady Lockheed!" the older woman declared. "What a pleasure it is to host you and your daughter. It has been an age since my last daughter was married off, you know, and I've had little excuse to make the rounds since then. I cannot wait to show you all around London!"

Auntie Frances smiled back with unexpected warmth, though there was a hint of nervousness behind the expression. "The pleasure is all ours, of course, Lady Hayworth," she said. "It's ever so gracious of you to allow us your time and attention." Auntie Frances turned back towards Vanessa, who had already dropped into a polite curtsy – this, despite the fact that they were all certainly stiff and miserable from the journey. "This is my daughter, Vanessa."

"It's so delightful to meet you, Lady Hayworth," Vanessa said, with the utmost sincerity in her tone. It was one of

Vanessa's charms, Dora thought, that she was always able to find *something* to be truly delighted about.

"Oh, how lovely you are, my dear!" the countess cried. "You remind me already of my youngest. You can be sure we shall be fighting off more suitors than we can handle in no time!" Lady Hayworth's eyes swept briefly over Dora, but then continued past her. Dora was wearing a dark, sturdy dress which must have made her appear as a very fine lady's maid, rather than as a member of the family. Lady Hayworth turned back towards the townhouse, beckoning them forward. "You must be awfully tired from the road," she said. "Please come inside, and we shall set a table—"

"This is my cousin, Theodora!" Vanessa blurted out. She reached out to grab Dora's arm, as though to make sure no one could mistake the subject of her introduction. The countess turned with a slight frown. Her gaze settled back upon Dora – and then upon her eyes. Lady Hayworth's warm manner cooled to a faint wariness as she took in the mismatched colours there.

"I see," the countess said. "My apologies. Lady Lockheed did mention that you might be bringing another cousin, but I fear that I quite forgot."

Dora suspected that Auntie Frances might have downplayed the possibility, in the hopes that Vanessa might change her mind before they left. But Lady Hayworth was quick to adjust, even if she didn't quite pause to finish the formal introduction.

Still, Lady Hayworth led them into a comfortable sitting room, where a maid brought them biscuits and hot tea while they waited for supper to finish being prepared. The countess and Auntie Frances talked for quite some time, gossiping about upcoming parties and the eligible bachelors who were known to be attending them. Dora found herself distracted by the sight of a tiny ladybird crawling across the knee of her gown. She was just thinking that she ought to sneak it outside before one of the maids noticed it, when Vanessa spoke and broke her out of her musings.

"And which parties will the Lord Sorcier be attending?" Dora's cousin asked the countess.

Lady Hayworth blinked, caught off-guard by the inquiry. "The Lord Sorcier?" she asked, as though she wasn't certain she'd heard Vanessa correctly. When Vanessa nodded emphatically, the countess frowned. "I admit, I do not know offhand," she said. "But whatever romantic notions you may have taken up about him, I fear that he will not be a suitable match for you, my dear."

"Why ever not?" Vanessa asked innocently over her tea. "He's quite young for the position of court magician, I hear, and very handsome as well. And is he not a hero of the war?" Dora heard a subtle, misleading note in her cousin's voice, however, and she studied Vanessa's face carefully, trying to pick apart what she was up to.

"That much is true," Lady Hayworth admitted. "But Lord Elias Wilder is really *barely* a lord. The Prince Regent insisted on giving him the French courtesy title, of course, with all those silly privileges that the French give their own court magicians. Technically, the Lord Sorcier may even sit in on the House of Lords. But his blood is common, and his manners are exceptionally uncouth. I have had the misfortune of encountering him on several occasions now. He has the face of an angel, and the tongue of some foul... *dockworker.*"

Dora found it amusing that the countess apparently considered dockworkers to be an appropriate foil for angels. She was briefly distracted by the notion that hell might be full of legions and legions of dockworkers, rather than devils.

"He does sound terribly unsuitable," Vanessa said reluctantly, regaining Dora's attention. "But please, if you don't mind – I would love to meet the Lord Sorcier at least once. I've heard such stories about him, and I would be crushed to leave London without even seeing him."

The countess tutted mildly. "I suppose we shall see," she said. "But for the very first thing, I have a wish to see you at Lady Carroway's ball. She has *many* fine and suitable sons, and you could do worse than entering London society at one of her parties…"

The subject meandered once again, until they were brought into dinner. They met Lord Hayworth that evening in passing, though he seemed quite busy with his own affairs, and less than interested in his wife's social doings. Once or twice, Dora thought to ask Vanessa about her interest in the Lord Sorcier, but her cousin kept demurring and changing the subject of conversation, and she eventually decided it was best to drop the matter while within current company.

Dora next thought that she would wait to ask until they were off to bed…but directly after dinner, she was swept away by a maid and given a hot bath, then bundled into a very lovely feather-down bed a few rooms down from her cousin.

Tomorrow, Dora thought distantly, while she stared at the foreign ceiling with interest. *I am sure we'll speak tomorrow.*

Quietly, she pulled the iron scissors from the sheath around her neck and tucked them beneath her pillow. As she drifted off to sleep, she dreamed of angels on the London docks, filing up and down the pier and hustling crates of tea onto ships.

if you enjoyed

THAT TIME I GOT DRUNK AND YEETED A LOVE POTION AT A WEREWOLF

look out for

A FEATHER SO BLACK

Fair Folk: Book One

by

Lyra Selene

In a kingdom where magic has been lost, Fia is a rare changeling, left behind by the wicked Fair Folk when they stole the high queen's daughter and locked the gates to the otherworld. Though most despise Fia's fae blood, the queen treats her as a daughter and trains her to be a spy. Meanwhile, the true princess, Eala, is bound to the otherworld, cursed to become a swan by day and only returning to her true form at night.

When a hidden gate to the otherworld is discovered, Fia is tasked by the high queen to retrieve Eala and break her curse. But she doesn't go alone: With her is Prince Rogan, Eala's betrothed and Fia's childhood best friend.

As the two journey into a world where magic winds through the roots of the trees and beauty can be a deadly illusion, Fia's mission is complicated by her feelings for the prince...and her unexpected attraction to the dark-hearted fae lord holding Eala captive. Irian might be more monster than man, but he seems to understand Fia in a way no one ever has.

Fia begins to question everything—the truth of her origins, the reality of her mission, and the motives of her mother, the high queen. But time is running out to break her sister's curse. And unraveling the secrets of the past and preserving the balance between the realms might destroy everything she loves.

Chapter One

Gort—Ivy

Autumn

I should not have drunk the blackberry wine. It slid violet through my veins and pricked sharp thorns at the nape of my neck. I'd thought it would calm me—focus my mind on the task at hand—but the opposite was true. I felt loose and reckless, jittering with nerves. I curled my hands tighter around my cup, fighting the brambles nettling at my fingertips.

Served me right for drinking on duty.

"More wine?" Connla Rechtmar, prince of Fannon, leaned forward in his fur-draped seat. He sloshed a carafe of purple liquid and flashed me an expectant smile. "Or do I need to offer you something stronger to make you take off that cloak you're hiding under?"

By now, the wine had traveled to my face, and I fought a flush—not of girlish embarrassment, but of fury. He had the audacity to speak to me like I was some timid strumpet? I could break his neck without breaking a sweat.

My wine-spiked blood pounded between my ears, hot with the prospect of violence.

I reminded myself that Connla didn't know what I was capable of. And if I had any sense, I'd keep it that way.

The tent was too warm, the fire roaring to ward off late autumn's chill. I would've preferred it cold—a bite of frost to keep me alert. I forced myself to count off the steps of my mission through the fevered muddle of my thoughts:

One. Get to the carafe of wine.

Two. Drug the wine.

Three. Smother Connla's unconscious face in his mound of seduction furs. (If I had time.)

Four. Find the prince's captive darrig.

Five. Bring the wicked creature to my mother.

I took a deep breath, even as I pressed a thumb against the bracelet I wore around my wrist, a woven circle of dried poison ivy, nettle, and bramble. It dug into the tender ring of irritated skin below it. The flare of pain untangled the snarl of my thoughts.

I undid the clasp of my heavy woolen cloak, dropping it

to the floor before my skin could prickle with sharp thorns. Without the outer garment, the air was blessedly cooler on my bare arms and exposed collarbones. I looked up through my lashes at Connla, gauging his reaction to my kirtle—or lack thereof. The sheer forest-green silk was striking against my pale skin and did little to disguise my physique. The thin shoulder straps were unnecessary considering how tight I'd cinched the bodice, accentuating my modest curves and slender waist. The high slit in the skirt left little to the imagination.

It achieved the desired effect. Connla's eyes widened, then darkened. He shifted in his chair. I fought the urge to shudder at the vulgar anticipation slicking his gaze.

Truthfully, I could have worn a grain sack or a few judiciously placed oak leaves. Connla wanted me, with or without the clinging dress, and I'd known it since that morning.

For the past fortnight, all the under-kings and noblemen of Fódla had been camped near Rath na Mara—the high queen's capital—to participate in the Áenach Tailteann, funeral games held to celebrate and mourn kings of Fódla. This year's assembly honored the late under-king of Eòdan and crowned his heir.

For the first few days, the high queen, Eithne Uí Mainnín—my adoptive mother—had presided over the creation of new laws, followed by a great funeral pyre in the king's honor. Then the games had begun—trials of physical and mental prowess that allowed young warriors and poets the opportunity to prove their strength, valor, and wit.

Connla Rechtmar had represented his father's household in a few categories—archery, horse racing, blades. He'd won all his matches—an odd bit of luck, considering he was lazy and slow, even for a prince.

Mother had not allowed me to compete. No—I was her secret, her instrument, her *weapon*. Flaunting my skills before her nobles was of no use to her—not if she wished me to spy on them, tease out their secrets, hunt down their weaknesses. So, as always, she kept me beside her in the queen's box, demurely dressed and diffident. The queen's favored fosterling—a strange, quiet little mouse.

That was where Connla noticed me. It wasn't unusual to feel eyes on the side of my face—even though I looked chaste and obedient, there were the rumors. There were *always* the rumors—about where I'd come from, why I looked the way I did, why the queen took particular interest in me. But Connla's regard was different—an oily kind of interest I didn't find particularly flattering. I was debating whether I could surreptitiously give him the two-fingered salute across the ring, when Mother leaned over to me. She pretended to tuck an errant lock of sable hair beneath my veil.

"Rechtmar's son desires you," she murmured to me, too quiet for her other attendants to hear.

"I noticed," I grumbled. And then, hopefully: "May I kill him for it?"

"You may not." She almost smiled. "Cathair?"

Ollamh Cathair—the queen's druid, chief advisor, and long-term lover—moved from his place behind her. He slid onto the bench beside me as Mother returned her attention to the archery contest below. His unwanted closeness chased away my cheekiness, but I forced myself not to flinch.

Cathair was a slender middle-aged man with a mild bearing. But his looks were his best deception. He had trained me in many things these past eleven years. Folklore. Ciphers. Poisons. Espionage. But first and foremost, he had taught me never to show my enemy how much I hated him.

"Fannon has been exceptionally lucky in their border skirmishes this year," Cathair muttered. "Flash floods sweeping away enemy troops, falling trees blocking supply wagons. That kind of thing. My informants believe they may have captured a darrig."

A finger of ice slid down my spine. It was expressly forbidden to consort with the Fair Folk. To keep a darrig was treason—the gnome-like creatures could predict events not yet passed and affect the outcome of simple occurrences. A tree falling, perhaps. The direction of a flood. Or even the outcome of a sword fight in a tournament.

"You believe Connla has the darrig?" I guessed, keeping my eye on the prince in question, who was celebrating his *lucky* wins by lazily swilling ale in the stands.

"Old Rechtmar is past his prime," Cathair told me. "Connla is his heir, his war advisor, and the captain of his fianna. If anyone has it, it will be Connla. Capture the thing for us, won't you?"

"You mean execute it." I glanced past Cathair to the queen. "Don't you?"

"Not this time." His expression held the kind of deadly intent I'd learned not to question. "We have a use for the creature."

I hid my uncertainty. Mother despised and distrusted the Fair Folk—they who had once ruled this land as gods. They were wicked, fickle, violent creatures who did not belong in the human realm. During a diplomatic delegation twenty years ago, the Folk had assassinated the high king, Mother's husband. The unjustified execution had incited the Gate War. The fight had been savage and bloody, until the Folk had effectively ended it by stealing away twelve human girls—the last, the queen's own daughter.

Mother *never* utilized the treacherous Folk for her own devices. Except me, the changeling child who had been left in her daughter's place twelve years ago. But after so much time in the queen's household, I was far more human than Folk. And everything I did for Mother, I did willingly.

Including this.

I refocused my attention on Connla, who was still staring brazenly at me from below. "How am I supposed to find the darrig?"

"You've demonstrated your tactical skills to me, little witch. And you've been developing an adequate head for subterfuge." Cathair's voice was sardonic. "But you have not yet proved yourself adept at seduction."

I wasn't thrilled by that idea. But what Cathair—and by extension, Mother—asked of me, I obeyed.

So here I was—a little drunk, sweating my arse off in a gown that left nothing to the imagination, as an overfed prince beckoned me closer with greedy fingers. Again, I fought a shudder of disgust.

I reminded myself this face did not belong to me. Nor the body, most likely. Who cared if I used them as tools, as *weapons*? They were nothing but what I made of them.

I swayed toward Connla, pasting on a slow smile and swinging my hips more than was strictly necessary. He patted his knee and I lowered myself onto his lap, gritting my teeth as his hand slithered around my waist.

"Yes, more wine is exactly what we need," I murmured, leaning into him. "But won't you allow *me* to serve *you* this time, my prince?"

I reached for the carafe of wine. But Connla caught my hand with one of his own, gripping my wrist. His eyes raked me from head to toe, bright with a canny light.

"I didn't expect your message tonight, *my lady*." His breath was hot and sour on my cheek. "Nor did I expect you to show up in my tent, half-dressed and eager for wine."

"What can I say?" I clenched my jaw harder behind my smile. "I couldn't take my eyes off you. Besides, it's hard to find a decent drink up at Rath na Mara."

"Perhaps. Or perhaps you had some other reason." His eyes glittered. "You see, after your unexpected note, I confess I told a few local lads about it. I maybe even bragged a bit. And what they had to say about you was...*interesting*."

His hand tightened around my wrist, sending pain flaring up my arm.

"The thing is, *Fia Ní Mainnín*, everyone says you're not actually a cousin of the queen. They say you're a little witch. A cailleach, if you can believe it." His voice took on an unpleasant note. "Now, I've lain with a witch or two before, so I couldn't care less about that. But they also say your power comes from the Folk. They say you're a *changeling*."

Shite.

"Changeling?" I forced a laugh, which came out reedy. "The wine must have addled your wits, my lord. I'm the queen's *foster*ling."

"I know what I heard." His expression was implacable. "You're unnatural. Look at you—your hair is dark as deep water. Your mismatched eyes are strange enough to give a man nightmares. You're small enough to snap like a twig in the forest. I'd wager money on it—you're a filthy changeling, like they said. Where did the high queen find you? How does she keep you? And what must I do to take you from her?"

I froze at the menace—the *hunger*—in Connla's voice. His grip on me tightened painfully. My options were narrowing by the moment. My veins itched with brambles, and I fantasized— brilliantly, achingly—of wrapping my fingers around his throat and choking him with thorns. Filling his mouth with sharp leaves, blanking his eyes with wet berries until I returned him to the land as a creeping, stinging blackberry bush.

It would be so easy.

But mother would eat my liver for breakfast if I Green-marked one of her under-kings' heirs without her say-so. With more willpower than I knew I possessed, I calmed myself.

Still, his words crept into my mind on serrated little feet.

You're small enough to snap like a twig in the forest.

The words rankled me, although they were half-true—I *was* small. I'd always been small. When Mother first sent me to her weapons masters to learn to ride and shoot and wrestle and fence, I was nine, and small even for my age. I couldn't draw the longbows favored by Mother's fianna; I couldn't reach the backs of their fine tall stallions; I couldn't even begin to lift the broad straight claimhte carried by proud fénnidi into battle. So I fashioned my own bows out of young saplings I found in the wood, and I taught myself to ride bareback on fleet marsh ponies too small for grown adults and to fight fast and dirty with a dagger in both hands. Even now, at twenty, I was small—shorter than most and lean from strict exercise and rigorous sparring.

But size wasn't everything. The height of a bow was worth less than the aim of the archer. The stride of a horse was worth less than its will to run. The length of a sword was worth less than the edge on its blade.

I was small. I was a changeling, although I'd be damned if I admitted it to this fatted prince. But I was fast and fierce and unrelentingly trained.

Screw the revealing dress and the subterfuge. I was going to have to do this my way.

Without warning, I jabbed my free hand inward, catching Connla's bicep above his elbow. He grunted as the muscle spasmed. His grip on my wrist relaxed—I wrenched my hand free and sucker punched him in the face. He reeled back, dumping me out of his lap. Blood dripped down his chin, staining the expensive rug under his feet.

"You bitch," he gasped wetly.

"Bitch, witch." I shrugged. "Just don't ever call me change-ling again."

I climbed him like a ladder before he could so much as make a fist. Wrapping both arms around his head, I swung my legs around his neck—the fabric of my dress audibly ripping—and threw myself backward. My weight jerked Connla forward, cartwheeling him head over arse. He landed hard on his back, the wind visibly gusting out of his chest.

I landed neatly on my feet. I crouched over him where he flailed like a gutted fish, planting my elbows on my knees and staring into his blood-drenched face.

"Tell me where the darrig is," I demanded.

It took him a long time to draw enough breath to say, "*No.*"

"Fine," I told him. "I'll find the wretched creature myself."

I slammed his skull against the edge of the fire pit. His eyes rolled back and his head lolled sideways.

The tent was large, but it wasn't endless. There were only so many places you could hide one of the Fair Folk, especially if you were keeping it captive. Somewhere out of the moonlight, which lent them power. Within a cage made of iron, which sapped their strength. I skipped the bed—mounded with soft furs, its purpose was revoltingly clear—and turned to Connla's war trunk.

Locked, of course. I could pick it, but that would take precious minutes I didn't have. Connla wouldn't be out for long.

I laid my hand against the mechanism, then hesitated.

Little witch.

When I was ten, I'd found an injured hedgehog at the edge of the forest. I snuck it into my chambers, hiding it beneath my bed. I'd come to adore it, nursing it back to health and naming it Pinecone. But I'd let it get too close to me. One day, I'd fallen asleep with it tucked against my chest, beneath my shirt. When I woke, my magic had taken Pinecone from me—all that remained were clods of dirt and flecks of blood held together by pine needles and wood sap.

Some people—Mother in particular—saw my magic as a gift. I knew it to be a curse. It never gave, only *took*.

Blood throbbed against my palm, dark with shadow and hot with wine. I hesitated a second longer, then closed my eyes. I imagined thick brambles studded with dark fruit and capped with sharp thorns. When I opened my eyes, tough briars had snaked into the mechanism.

The metal groaned, bent. Snapped. I threw the trunk open.

At first, it looked like Connla's trunk was full of jumbled sticks. But I blinked, and it was the darrig—a hunched and broken creature, with a body like a stump and limbs like gnarled branches and eyes like glossy pebbles. The iron cage Connla kept it in was too small—the darrig's legs didn't have room to bend without touching the metal, and ugly welts vied for space with bruises on its tree-bark skin. The sickening stench of burnt wood and rotting mulch wafted out of the trunk.

"Help," the darrig croaked.

orbit

Follow us:

/orbitbooksUS

/orbitbooks

/orbitbooks

Join our mailing list
to receive alerts on our
latest releases and deals.

orbitbooks.net

Enter our monthly
giveaway for the chance
to win some epic prizes.

orbitloot.com